Sub-Marine

To my brothers who walked with me on foggy shores and through Sub Port halls long before the writing of this book.

Chapter One
An Introduction

Two boys once lived by the sea.

Their names were Jack and Sam Wesley. They loved to be by the ocean and hurried down to the shore on most days. Visiting the coast was never a difficult endeavor for the two, for they lived on an island. This was not a tropical island, nor a tundra island, but a foggy, misty island that rested contentedly off the American northwest coast in the gloomy Pacific. Genoa.

It was a special place where all the people knew each other's names. At a large bay, an assortment of watercraft would have been found. Most of the island's visitors came during the summer months and stayed in boats since there were no inns on the island. Those who called Genoa home lived in cabins and makeshift shelters near the bay. At a family-run bar, sea-weathered men listened to radios and smoked cigars and drank cheap alcohol. A rickety stand at the harbor's port was where the residents could purchase cabbage, carrots, blueberries, and other fresh imports. A man by the name of Wheaton Edwards captained an ocean liner in Oregon and offered ferry service twice a week. This simple way of living was all that the people wanted.

For Jack and Sam, life was rarely ever boring. Despite the somewhat dreary weather, the two brothers had plenty to do. Fishing was Jack's favorite pastime, while Sam preferred to explore the island's oceanside caves. (A surprising number of these deep, watery caverns were found on Genoa.)

On a typical day, after reading or writing and doing their required chores, the two would bicycle to the beach. Usually with some friends, Jack and Sam would glide past the town park, seemingly always littered with the most brilliant red and orange fallen leaves, and over the quiet stream in Whitefield Garden where trout lazily meandered along. Then, the comrades would traverse one of the several routes to the west coast of the island where a stretch of muddy hills dipped into the sea. This special place was a place of youthful jubilation. Amid a dense, green forest, the youngsters hiked, climbed trees, and occasionally swam in the icy pebble-bottom river.

Jack and his friends threw footballs on the beach and met in elaborate tree forts to trade fishing lures and model planes. Sam, the leader of cave exploration, would guide the most daring children into dark, damp tunnels and through small apertures in the beach's rocky regions.

At the day's end, as the orange sun fell below the wind-beaten ocean, they would all hastily disperse and scurry northward for dinner.

Aside from these thrilling escapades, Jack and

Sam enjoyed their life at home. Two stories tall, built with large wooden frames, their house was originally a fishing-supply store. The boys' parents had worked hard to make the place a pleasant home; the couple had made the larger rooms into an observatory, a kitchen, and a library. It was a welcoming place, and the Wesleys' neighbors visited often.

Like any other children living on Genoa, Jack and Sam didn't go to school because the population was much too small for a public institution to be built. Nevertheless, the two were well educated. Constantly reading old books they uncovered in the "Wesley Library", these students were two of the island's best. Jack was a writer and would journal about their adventuresome quests, while Sam was undeniably creative and loved to build things.

In many ways, the two took after their father. John Wesley, their brilliant though slightly eccentric father, was an established engineer. He had grey hair and wore spectacles most of the time. Before Jack and Sam were born, John and his wife Marie moved to Genoa. He had been invited to work for Incandium Science Labs, a very exclusive and highly sophisticated group of scientists. Dr Lewis Verne, the company's president, had learned of John's competence and wished for him to assist the laboratory.

As you will see, John's work was altogether secretive; the president obliged him to keep from speaking about the details of his business. Because of this, his children had quite the mystery on their hands. The part that especially confused them was *where* their father worked. For many years, the location of the scientists' workplace was wholly unknown to the brothers.

Jack and Sam would often go on undisclosed treks to search for the place. All that the two ever found was a military bunker from the Second World War and an abandoned camping trail. Of course, the two never dared venture to the southern tip of the island; the children of Genoa believed an evil vagabond lived there and that he carried a dagger with him. Due to the obscurity of the laboratory, Jack and Sam merely knew that their father had an important job at a concealed location and was *extremely* busy with it.

John had known Marie Hudson since he was a boy. The two were raised in Oregon, in the same little town. The teenager had never met someone so wonderful. Marie was beautiful in appearance, but the Oregonian high schooler had loved her for her heart; he saw that Marie was constantly looking for ways to help others. Unlike John, she sought excitement and accepted uncertainty.

Jack and Sam were born on Genoa and raised by the sweetest of mothers. Taking them on boat rides and morning walks, Marie taught her sons to use their imaginations because, as she said, "imagination leads to adventure."

She once happened upon a crippled, poor man on a winter evening. Taking him in for the night, Marie actually saved the man from freezing to death. Though she abhorred any recognition, she was constantly considered a hero because of her noble efforts.

In the fall of nineteen thirty-nine, Marie became ill from a rampant disease that had been introduced to Genoa. John sought day and night to find the right treatment, but there was little available for her on the small island. He gave her medicine of all sorts and fed her the best food he could find, but his wife grew sicker with each new day.

Desperate to save her, John wished that there was some way to change what had happened; he dreamt of a world where his wife never became sick, a world without variability.

A few long and bitter days later, Marie died in her sleep. This event marked the beginning of the darkest chapter of John's life; he became utterly depressed and endeavored to seek an escape from his anguish through work.

Jack and Sam were still young when their mother passed away, and it was a perilous challenge for their father to explain to them what had happened. Though they missed her immensely, the two became accustomed to getting along on their own.

John was given some time off at Incandium, and Jack and Sam quickly noticed that something was dreadfully different about the man. His hair turned grey and his spirit, dark. During his break, John hired a man named David Berkley to watch after his children while he would be gone at Incandium.

Mr Berkley was Genoa's lighthouse operator and was known for his pleasant and relaxed demeanor. He had brown hair and a weathered face and usually wore a bright-blue vest that matched his bold, blue eyes. While he was known to have been athletic and rather striking in his youth, his latter years found him somewhat portly but notably kindhearted. He lived on the north-east peninsula of the island in his simple cottage. The home was adjoined to the magnificent red and white lighthouse that protruded from smooth sun-bleached rocks. Mr Berkley once proudly explained to Jack and Sam that he was the first man to take permanent residence on Genoa. The two were suspicious about his claim, although they *were* told by others that he had come to the island as a child.

As an academic enthusiast, Mr Berkley enjoyed teaching the Wesleys about all sorts of things. Whether through expounding on American history or by teaching the two how to tie knots, he seemed always eager to offer his abundant knowledge. The two became recognized as scholarly individuals and received remarks like, "You make the king's jive!" and, "Are you writing a book?" They wholly aspired to be like Mr Berkley, a chap of surprising knowledge and sought-after wisdom.

Because Mr Berkley was good friends with the ocean liner captain (as he was with most folk in the area), he and the Wesleys were given a free ride to the mainland harbor each summer. Although Jack enjoyed the tradition, he was consistently disappointed because he had always wanted to travel further east; he wanted dearly to know what life would be like on prairies and in mountains.

You might find it humorous that Genoa's renowned lighthouse man was entirely opposed to getting married; he simply didn't see the need. Jack and Sam sometimes teased him about his position, but, to their dismay, he was skilled at making fun of himself. Mr Berkley found all of his joy in Genoa and in helping its people.

Mr Berkley was a regimented man and rarely ever did he deviate from his daily routines. After a slow morning, he would drive his station wagon to the Wesleys' home. There, he would say hello to the boys and look after any important tasks. Once the things were in order, he would join the two in their activities, educating them along the way. He would often take the brothers hiking along the white rocks on the eastern shoreline. It was there that they would hunt pheasants, trading around Mr Berkley's old shotgun. The lighthouse man never failed to supply the Wesleys plenty of food and things. Each afternoon, the blue-vested islander would take the dusty road back to his cottage. Before his nightly lighthouse duty, he would take a nap and then eat supper. As evening turned to dusk, he would climb a long spiral staircase to the top of his red and white tower. Throughout his nights, Mr Berkley would always give careful attention to his trusty radio which allowed him to communicate with Captain Edwards. He took much pride in his magnificent lighthouse and kept it in quite perfect shape, shining its brilliant beam of light wherever needed.

Jack and Sam became exceptionally fond of the

easygoing lighthouse man. You see, the brothers were the only children who had grown up and continued to live on the island. The other children came and went, staying for only a few years at most. Like the Wesley children, Mr Berkley was there to stay.

Shortly after returning to work, John found himself in a new position at Incandium. Now, he was gone more than ever. Living at the laboratory, he would only visit home on certain occasions. Although his children were extremely upset about their father's absences, they aimed to spend time with him and tell him all about their schooling and adventures. John continued to be shadowy and reserved about his work and told his boys that it was for their own good that he keep quiet. This, of course, made them all the more curious; they became determined to learn anything they could about Incandium Science Labs. Despite their father, Jack and Sam began to use the clues they found to solve their mystery.

John loved his children and enjoyed being with them, but his vocation was clearly his priority. Mr Berkley wasn't blind to the harm being done and eventually confronted his friend, being terribly frustrated with him for leaving the children on their own. Despite his exasperation, Mr Berkley found that John would not change his ways.

To Jack and Sam, their father seemed conflicted, struggling to navigate between his family and his work. As they grew older, the Wesley boys carried on with their delightful exploits. However, they became increasingly worried about their troubled father.

Although Mr Berkley adored the engineer's children, his patience with their vanishing father would run out. Perplexed by John Wesley and his absences, Mr Berkley was to face his greatest challenge yet and to become the hero that his island would need.

Chapter Two
A Significant Discovery

Our story begins in December, on a particularly chilly night. Jack and Sam were camping on a hill near the island's peninsula. At the time, Jack was fifteen years old, and Sam, seventeen. The two were seeking a novel quest; dare I say they were becoming somewhat weary of Genoa. They had planned this to be their final camping trip of the season since the weather was becoming increasingly unpleasant. Their father had been gone for some time now, and it didn't help at all that they had independently sensed a strange and unfamiliar aura throughout Genoa.

The sky was dark-red when the Wesleys awoke. Quietly collecting their fishing rods and tackle boxes, they left to go fishing at a small lake beside the hill. As they sat down on a flat boulder, the gloomy clouds rolled away and the morning sun appeared, lethargically illuminating the water with warm beams. It was wintertime, and the color in the town park's fallen leaves was fading quickly.

Jack had forgotten to bring gloves on the camping trip and was relieved when the sun emerged from behind the hill. After undoing a knot in his fishing line, he said, "I heard Chad is moving back to the mainland."

"Did ya'?" his brother responded. "I was sure he'd stay 'till spring at least."

"They say his parents need more work." Jack said, playing with his reel. "We should go to the mainland next month—just you and me. I'd love to see that atomic bomb exhibition by the harbor."

"You know Mr Berkley wouldn't allow it." Sam stated sternly.

"He's got to let us off the island once in a while! We're not children anymore." As Jack said this, his pole bent towards the water. "I've got one!" he remarked.

Sam helped his brother take a wiggling bass off a sharp hook. "Nice catch." he said.

Jack was an experienced fisher and casually stated that the fish wasn't "*that* big." He placed it back in the water and the two left the lake. Then, they packed their tent, rolled up their sleeping bags, and began bicycling home.

As they rode down a rocky slope, they passed by the lighthouse.

Jack was surprised to see that Mr Berkley's station wagon was missing. "Where's he off to so early?" he thought.

The two glanced at the ocean before taking a trail that cut across the point.

"'Ya' see how low the tide was?" Sam inquired, motioning towards the wavy sea.

"Yeah, I did." Jack answered, getting back onto his

bicycle without giving the observation much consideration.

A while later, the two arrived at their home, and Mr Berkley's car was there, parked between their porch and a towering oak tree.

"He came early!" Sam declared.

They left their camping equipment by their front door and came inside. Jack was wondering what had caused Mr Berkley to alter his fixed routine.

"Mr Berkley?" Sam called, stepping into a quiet living room.

The lighthouse man's voice came from the observatory: "I've been looking all over for you two. Where have you been?"

Coming to the stairway, Jack asked, "You didn't see the note we left? We were camping."

The man's eyes twinkled. "My apologies," he said, brushing a pink hand through his brown hair, "I must not have seen your note in my busyness."

The brothers ascended into the observatory and Sam said, "Mr Berkley, why you are here so early?"

The lighthouse man, who was holding something in his hands, seemed troubled, which was a rare sight. The boys sat down on stools because Mr Berkley seemed to have important news. He too sat down and told his story: "Last night, I was expecting the *Jolly Tempus* to arrive at our port at midnight, as was planned. I can usually sight the liner from a mile away, but the sea was quiet just before twelve. I thought this was strange, so I radioed Edwards—but he didn't respond. This gave me the zorros; you boys know that my radio never fails me." Mr Berkley shook his head and explained, "I was frantic. I telephoned the mainland services, but they would not respond either! I waited for hours, and I knew something was seriously wrong." The man was squirming on his stool. "I began sending distress signals on my radio, and then, early this morning, I received a telegram!"

"A telegram?" repeated Sam.

Mr Berkley wore a serious face and nodded. He then held up a piece of paper. "It came from Edwards at Hester Bay." he said, before giving the message to the two.

"HESTER BAY OREGON

"SEVERE STORM ALERT

"445 AM PST SUN DEC 09 1951

"A NEW STORM TRANSITIONS INTO CATE-GORY FOUR HURRICANE

"IT MOVES NORTH-NORTHWESTWARD TOW-ARD GENOA ISLAND

"CURRENT LOCATION ROUGHLY 43N 124W ABOUT 15 MI 24 KM ESE OF LYN FIELD BAY

"MAXIMUM SUSTAINED WINDS 140 MPH 225 KMH

"PRESENT MOVEMENT WNW 15 DEGREES AT 6MPH 10 KMH

"JOLLY TEMPUS FORCED TO REROUTE

"STORM DISABLED ALL VESSEL COMMU-NICATIONS

"HURRICANE DEVELOPMENT WAS UNFORE-SEEN

"COURSE HAS UNEXPLAINABLY CHANGED AND STORM HAS INCREASED IN STRENGTH

"REGULAR PASSAGE UNADVISED DUE TO STROM INTENSITY

"YOU HAVE TWENTY HOURS TO EVACUATE

"BOARD ANY AVAILABLE SEA CRAFT AND TRAVEL SOUTH

"THIS SYSTEM WILL DESTROY EVERYTHING ON GENOA ISLAND

"THIS IS A DEADLY STORM

"BEST OF LUCK TO MY DEAREST ISLAND FRIENDS

"CAPTAIN EDWARDS OF THE JOLLY TEMPUS"

The brothers read the telegram and then looked to Mr Berkley with dread.

"What are we going to do?" whispered Jack.

The lighthouse man grimly stated, "We will evacuate the island."

"But, *where* could we possibly go?" Sam cried.

Mr Berkley stood up and Jack observed on his face a hopeful expression that he would wear when he had something significant to reveal. "For some time," the lighthouse man said, "your father and I have kept a box of important emergency supplies: life vests, ocean charts, navigational instruments, an alarm system, and things like that. John came up with the plan to open the box if the island ever became unsafe. So, when the telegram came in this morning, I went to get the box from my basement. But, when I opened it, I found something!"

Mr Berkley rushed to a desk and the brothers

followed. There, on the desktop, lay a detailed map of Genoa. On the south side of the island, an "X" and some coordinates were written. And, at the top-right corner of the page, a series of numbers was also written: "5813."

"I found this map lying on top of the supplies, and with it came an important message." Mr Berkley stated, revealing a torn piece of paper from his vest pocket. "Listen to this:

"'Mr Berkley,

"'I'm leaving you this map for your safety. A situation has developed and I will be at Incandium indefinitely. I can't explain it, but I'm afraid we might have put the island in danger. If Genoa is struck by an unusual storm, use this map to get the people to safety. Please make it your priority to protect Jack and Sam. I'm not allowed to share these coordinates, but I no longer have a choice.

"'I dearly hope this never becomes necessary.

"'Your friend, John'"

They were all overwhelmed by the news; the three had never been in such dire circumstances. In silence, each brother examined the note.

"You'd never seen this map before?" asked Sam.

"Not once." Mr Berkley replied. He looked up and then down and then said, "When your father was last here, he and I added some supplies to the box. He must have placed this inside without me knowing it."

"How could father have known that this was going to happen?" Jack pondered. He was entirely puzzled about the whole development.

The brothers soon asked Mr Berkley if he had yet visited the place designated on the map. He said that he hadn't and that he planned to take them there immediately. Shortly after the discussion, the three agreed to visit this southern location. Although their situation was unfortunate, the map was certainly good news to the three. Jack, Sam, and Mr Berkley collected their things and, after loading the automobile, set out on what was to become their most incredible adventure.

Chapter Three
The Beginning of an Adventure

A breeze from the west. Billowy clouds. Birds in flight, constantly in flight. It was undeniable that a storm was on its way. Mr Berkley was prepared for a storm—he was always prepared. But *this* was not merely a storm. This kind of storm had never before met Genoa's shores.

"The coordinates lead to Miller's Park." Jack remarked, studying the map.

The tide was astonishingly low as Mr Berkley and the Wesley boys took a bumpy dirt road to the south corner of the island.

"I wonder what we'll find there." Sam whispered.

Jack declared, "I bet we'll find the laboratory."

"Whatever we find, let's hope it will get us far from the island." Mr Berkley said. He was surely worried; John's letter was perfectly vague and he had plenty of trouble trusting that they would find "safety" at the southern tip.

A short time later, the three arrived at a forest called Miller's Park. The place had been closed for many years, ever since a rockslide blocked off the entryway with sharp branches and massive rocks. Mr

Berkley parked on the side of the road and the boys brought out some bags.

Avoiding the treacherous entryway, the three jumped an old wooden fence by the road and detoured around the forest trail. Creaky trees swayed in an unfamiliar wind as they went by.

Sam and Mr Berkley were being cautious, but Jack excitedly rushed towards the shore. While running down the steep incline, he took a fall, nearly stumbling into a deep crevasse hidden by some bushes. "Jiminy!" he shouted, standing up and looking down into the seemingly bottomless hole. "Look out for the gap, fellas!"

The three passed by the cleft and came to the edge of the forest. After trudging through some brambly bush, Jack found himself in a vast, overgrown plain. The sky was mostly grey and the ocean breeze was fierce. He briefly felt the warmth of the sun before an angry gust blew the hat off his head.

Coming out of the woods, Sam remarked, "It's only a field," and asked for further directions.

Mr Berkley showed him the map and explained, "Now, we will make a turn here and then go towards the point."

Now that Jack was in the vicinity of the south peninsula, he began thinking of the vagabond, ole' Benny. The grass was tall and the wildlife, undisturbed. As birds chirped nearby, he was surprised to have found a place on Genoa he hadn't yet explored. "Mr Berkley," he said, "have you been here before?"

"I came to this place many times as a teenager,"

the lighthouse man said, staring intently towards the ocean, "when I began my lighthouse work, I stopped coming, and I haven't been back since." He looked at the map, changed direction slightly, and then said, "A while ago, I heard a story about a man who came here to look for a gemstone and was never seen again."

After passing some pine trees, the group came to a gravel road. This was strange, for the three hadn't known of any roads on the south shore.

"Let's follow it!" cried Sam.

They began running. The road was leading them towards the "X."

"I see something," Mr Berkley announced, breathing heavily, "don't you? It's a car!"

The group halted and, standing on a dirt mound, sighted a blue automobile parked under a short pine tree. The gravel road bent eastward, towards a faraway hill. The ocean now lay directly ahead. As Jack and Sam came closer, they realized that the vehicle was their father's. The Wesleys swung their fists in excitement, for they were certain Incandium was as good as found.

"Mr Berkley, it's his roadster!" Jack shouted, pointing out the sleek blue car.

The lighthouse man then asked a logical question: "*Where* is the place we're looking for?" Standing where they believed the "X" to be, our explorers were perplexed, for there wasn't a building in sight.

The partners began walking about, looking for anything that could be counted as "safety" as John had put it. A rocky formation was seen off to the west and an arching hill rested between the blue roadster and the grey sea. Jack followed the sound of roaring waves. The hill became a cliff quite suddenly, dropping off into the water. He walked back and found his two companions standing beside the rocky formation. Coming closer, he saw that they had found a cave there.

"Do you think there might be anything inside?" Sam asked, peering into the small, dark opening.

"There's only one way to find out!" Mr Berkley answered, turning on his bulky flashlight and abruptly walking in.

Jack thought of ole' Benny and about the man Mr Berkley said had disappeared. "I'm not going in *there*." he thought. His brother left him, slipping into the rocky mouth.

Jack stood impatiently in the wet grass. He walked away and peered into his father's car. A liquor bottle lay in the passenger seat.

Growing restless, Jack entered the cave. The chamber smelled faintly of bat droppings. Something moved outside the cave and sent Jack running. "I'm coming!" he yelled as he was consumed by blackness. A moment later, he saw a dim light far inside the tunnel. He followed it best he could. The room became much larger once he was further inside. "That's odd." he thought. His two friends were found standing at the end of the chamber.

"There you are," Mr Berkley said, "see what we've found." He motioned to a heavy metal door which lay within the rocky extremity of the cave.

When Sam tried the door, a combination lock prevented him from entering. "We're locked out." he asserted, examining the rectangular device.

Jack was bewildered by the finding. He wiped the sweat from his face and then remembered something. "The numbers on the map–the set of numbers!"

A grinning face beamed at the boy. "Of course, Jack!" Mr Berkley's satchel opened and then closed, and the map was revealed. "Five eight one three!" read the man enthusiastically.

Sam lined up the numbers and the lock fell off the handle. Then, the door creaked open, slowly swinging on hinges rusted by salty air. Jack, Sam, and Mr Berkley were curious to see what lay beyond the secret passage. Their leader stepped aside as the Wesley brothers nervously passed into a deep darkness.

"What have we found?" asked Sam to himself.

Mr Berkley came beside the two. The man's silver beam bounced off the ceiling high above their heads and across the room's walls which were barely visible from the entrance. The reverberation in the cold air and the striking blackness proved that they were in a truly *massive* expanse. The three walked down a steep staircase, their footsteps echoing.

"Is anyone there?" shouted the chief explorer, his breath puffing misty condensation. Silence. The three understood that they were alone. "What is that?" asked Mr Berkley, walking towards a round and shiny surface. The brothers followed their elderly companion towards a soft sound of lapping water.

"A submarine!" shouted Jack in utter disbelief.

Resting in the black water, the metal vessel simply amazed the three adventurers. They had found the sail, the narrow part that protrudes from the top. Jack glimpsed the hull of the boat, sitting right below the water's surface. The level of the water puzzled Jack, as he was sure they were above sea level. He *had* read about pioneering docks that could be lowered and raised to protect from a rough ocean.

"There are more!" yelled Sam from a distance.

The lighthouse man aimed his flashlight towards the feverish lad. He pointed out three additional submarines, each docked beside a wooden platform.

"A well-kept secret indeed." proclaimed Mr Berkley, before his beam disappeared. "Oh, no. The flashlight's out of power."

"There must be some lights in here," Sam said, "let's look around."

Sam and Mr Berkley cautiously navigated the perimeter of the boathouse, feeling in the dark with their numb hands. Jack searched along the docks and soon happened upon a stock of glass lanterns that were lying on a round, metal table.

These were unlike any lanterns you or I have ever seen; they had a clear liquid inside of them, and when Jack flipped a small switch on the top of one, the whole thing shone with a brilliant, blue light. He almost dropped the glass article at first, then handled it cautiously, noticing that, despite its intense brightness, the lantern didn't give off any heat.

Of course, My Berkley and Sam were mystified by the discovery when they saw it themselves. Soon enough, they each carried one of these blue lanterns and, with much more efficiency, carried on with the investigation.

Amazed by the unavoidable presence of the mystifying monstrosities, the brothers revisited a submarine. They observed that its exterior was scarlet red and that there was one window in each side of the sail. When Jack took his lantern up to one of the portholes, he sighted a small table, a lamp, and a purple rug inside. Across the submarine floor he saw a ladder and a clock. Sam looked in as well and was equally intrigued. Large silver clamps on the dock kept the submarine in place, latching onto the front and back.

There was much to see inside the extraordinary boathouse, so the brothers moved on. Found on the concrete floor were strange contraptions and devices. Among the devices was what seemed to be a giant, triangular metal robot. Standing on five multi-jointed legs, the abstruse, deactivated machine awed the guests. "This is strange." declared Sam, noticing an inscription upon the upper half of the robot. "'S.A.P.' I wonder what that might mean."

Mr Berkley soon found a lever on the east wall, and after he pulled it, the entire room became visible; the ceiling was furnished with rows of the same kind of blue lights they had already found.

"What a charge!" Jack exclaimed, beholding the

expanse in an ultramarine-blue light. "This place is wild." He and his two companions noticed that, although there were four submarines, a fifth dock lay empty. Jack later concluded that his father had taken out the submarine that belonged to the vacant dock.

There were small billboards hanging on the walls, advertising various things: "Spring Cleaning at the Sub Port!", "Progress", and "Incandium Science Labs: at the Forefront of Undersea and Fire-Resistant Technology." These clues interested them, although they didn't understand what they meant. One billboard read, "Wesley and Verne Research," and the three were bewildered to see that John had earned a title with the company's president. Mr Berkley and the boys had never met Dr Verne and knew very little about him.

A trail of oil had been spilled along a deck, a few desks were scattered about the dusty floor, and one of John's jackets hung on the wall near the entrance.

It was now afternoon and, since they hadn't eaten all day, the three happily agreed to fetch their food. They exited the boathouse because they had left their bags by the roadster. As they discussed their situation on the hillside, dark clouds approached from the east like galloping war horses in eccentric, medieval fashion.

Sitting on a little rock, Sam asked, "Where are all the people?" He waved his hat towards the nearby cave. "This facility is *clearly* run by Incandium, but it isn't equipped for research. The scientists must work somewhere else."

"I agree," responded Mr Berkley, thoughtfully, "Incandium's workers must use these submarines as transport to their *main* research facility."

Jack took a bite from his apple and then said, "I'm sure glad we found this place, but how will we evacuate all the people?"

Mr Berkley was silent for a moment and then said, "All we have at the port are fishing boats, so we will have no chance sailing out there when the hurricane hits." He pointed towards the violent sea. "But, this is an exceptional shelter. I know your father has given us the coordinates for a good reason. He might have wanted the people to take shelter here, but I wonder–maybe he wanted us to come to Incandium!"

Sam certainly wanted to go. Jack was fearful and unsure.

"Either way, this is where we will take the people," the lighthouse man stated, "if we can't use the subs, we'll hide out down there during the storm. Do you understand?"

The two nodded.

"We will do a thorough check of all these vessels for fuel, food, and information. Then, we will warn the people."

Chapter Four
The Submarines

Rain began to descend in Miller's Park as Jack, Sam, and Mr Berkley dashed back inside the boat-house. The submarines awaited, shining in blue iridescence. Each dock consisted of a rectangular platform built upon a rocky foundation that plunged deep into the murky ocean water. The platforms were found to be blocked from the sea; as assumed by Jack, they maintained a water level much higher than the ocean's.

Chills crawled across Jack's skin as he grasped and climbed a series of curved steel bars up the side of a submarine. His two friends followed.

The three collectively wrenched open a circular hatch-door on the top of the sail. When the hatch came open, Mr Berkley abruptly slipped backwards. Jack grabbed his wrist, but the man was quite heavy for him to tug; the two began to tumble. Sam quickly grabbed Jack's waist to keep them from falling into the water. He pulled very hard and they all fell in a heap on the sail.

"Sorry lads," said the startled elder, slowly standing back up, "I should be more careful." Jack agreed, but didn't say so. The hatch was now opened and a wood ladder emerged from a new darkness.

A lantern was brought out and the three cautiously ventured down. The clock ticked and tocked on the wall beside them. There was the lamp and the small table and the purple rug. Mr Berkley searched for the power.

The passageway was narrow and the three were bumping against each other. The lighthouse man soon opened a square panel on the wall and figured that it operated the electronics. A loud alarm began to shriek when Mr Berkley flipped a switch. "Oh, that's not it!" he shouted, hurriedly turning the switch back off. Jack and Sam laughed.

Another switch was flipped and the room was immediately brightened, dancing in bright and beautiful colors. The walls were red and had white patterns painted all about them. The steel floor made a loud noise when walked on and the room smelled faintly of must. A spinning metal tube hung from the ceiling; it was a periscope and Sam enjoyed looking into it.

"Come on!" Jack implored, coming to a spiral staircase at the end of the room.

As the three came down, a distant trickle of reso-nance was heard echoing up the stairway. Jack believed he was hearing a tune.

Coming off the last step, Mr Berkley gasped. A finely furnished living area gleamed before them in lustrous allure. Innumerable glass beads dangling from a chandelier cast light about the room. Two wooden desks and four metal tables stood symmetrically along the sides of a long, elliptic carpet in the middle of the floor. Deep cabinets built into the walls lined each side of the submarine. Portholes looked into dark-green water and an American flag hung on the wall to the right.

"Wow!" exclaimed Sam, gesturing with his hands.

"What kind a' boat is this?" said Mr Berkley, wiping dust off a table.

Covered with red wallpaper portraying gold flowers, the walls were rounded, forming a semi-circular shape. The floor was metal, but the decorative carpet covered its majority.

"This place is nice!" declared Jack, casually falling into a cushioned chair beside a table.

Mr Berkley, who was focused on their plan, said, "I'll look for the control room. I think it's in the front."

The garnished living area was now left to the bewildered Wesley boys. Perhaps the most perplexing thing was the absence of sizable instruments and devices throughout the vessel. The two had seen pictures of tightly packed naval submarines, but *this* was totally different. Opening cabinet drawers, they found charts, journals, and a few small instruments.

Sam was interested by something in particular: hung above a desk, a vellum illustration depicted the south shore of Genoa and, below it, a large building. The long structure lay below a stream of blue waves. Written at the top of the page, in cursive, was "The Sub Port." He felt the rough surface of the paper with his hand. "Could this be the place we are looking for?" he thought aloud. "It seems as though it's underwater!"

"An underwater laboratory?" questioned Jack, rushing to examine the finding. *That's* impossible." He looked carefully at the intricate diagram. "The Sub Port." he whispered under his breath.

The two were still staring at the map when they heard Mr Berkley calling from a distance. "We're coming!" hollered Sam, rolling up the picture and taking it with him.

The brothers went through a heavy metal door with a turn-wheel and came to a hall where a half-turn staircase lead to a lower floor. Growing louder, a jazzy vibraphone tune invited the brothers deeper into the enthralling, sub-aquatic shelter. Another chandelier hung above them and some long metal tubes ran across the ceiling. The walls showcased more flowery wallpaper, and tall lamps stood at either end of the hall. Mr Berkley was seen in the next room, so they passed the stairs and went through another metal door.

The opposite sides of the submarine came together where the hull of the control room was almost completely glass. Unlike the others, this room's palette was sapphire-blue and white. A number of those same blue fixtures emitted light from the ceiling, while green lamps were positioned about the curved control board. Jack thought the chamber smelled like the library at his house.

Sitting in front of the large window, the lighthouse

man called the two over, saying, "Jack, Sam, I've found the controls." The board was coated with switches and flashing lights. Mr Berkley was looking intently at a glass display in the middle of the ocean of electronics. To the left of the display lay an arrangement of buttons: mostly letters and some commands. "See here. Look at this wonder." he said, showing the two that when he pressed a button with a letter on it, the respective text appeared on the screen.

Jack and Sam realized that the "wonder" Mr Berkley had found was a computer. At the time, computing apparatuses were extremely rare and almost only owned by large corporations. The three were intrigued.

Sam asked what the computer could do.

"I'm not entirely sure." the man admitted. Picking up a thin, lime-colored pamphlet, he said, "This may help."

Jack had at least read about such machines and gladly accepted the bright book labeled "Auto Pilot Manual." He read that the computer was programmed to respond to commands and found a collection of its prompts at the back of the pamphlet. Sitting beside Mr Berkley on a swivel chair, he referenced the manual, slowly typed "WELCOME", and then pressed the "Execute" button. Silence. Then, a small speaker above the control panel produced a crackle and a buzz.

A man's voice abruptly filled the blue and green control room: "Welcome to Incandium Transportation. I am your Auto Pilot, D.S.J. One Zero One Five. I am here to pilot this submarine and provide you with information. Please identify yourself using the keyboard."

The unknowing lighthouse man was quickly on his feet, searching for whom the voice belonged to. He saw his companions motioning to the cone-shaped intercom above the panel. "It came from there?" he asked, completely mystified by the unseen responder. The brothers assured him that they were still alone and he sat back down cautiously.

"It told us to identify ourselves," Jack recalled to his two companions, "let's put in father's name."

Sam nodded. Jack carefully typed out "JOHN WESLEY" and the clear and mysterious voice said, "Welcome, Dr Wesley."

"I've heard about computers," said Jack, "but one that can *talk*—that's unheard of!"

Sam snatched the pamphlet from his brother. "Jack! Look here." Sitting down between his companions, he pointed to a prompt on the list that read "SUB PORT INFORMATION."

Jack showed Mr Berkley the rendering of the Sub Port that they had found, describing the new theory about Incandium's location. This time, Sam typed the command.

"The Sub Port is the official headquarters of Incandium Science Labs," the Auto Pilot explained, "its purpose is to provide a laboratory and housing for the company's employees. Established in nineteen thirty-three by Dr Verne, this underwater masterpiece provides a secluded location for research on our various inventions."

Jack wondered what these "inventions" were. He remembered the billboards that he had seen.

"'Nineteen thirty-three.'" repeated Mr Berkley.

"This has got to be where father is!" Sam declared, pointing back to the picture.

"ROUTES AND FUNCTIONS" was the next command to try.

"Our submarines travel between the Sub Port, Port Verne, and Genoa Harbor," the Auto Pilot described, "Dr Verne has intended for Incandium's members to use my auto-piloting functions to ensure a safe and easy trip.

"The voyage between Genoa Harbor and the Sub Port lasts two days, while the voyage between Port Verne and the Sub Port lasts three days. If you wish to travel between Port Verne and Genoa Harbor, the submarine will need to stop at the Sub Port for refueling. The voyage is completely automated, except for the take-off and landing procedures."

"We're in luck," cheered Sam, "it seems that we won't have to pilot the submarines ourselves!"

Mr Berkley thanked God and Jack forced a smile.

"I wonder what Port Verne is." Sam stated before looking to the pamphlet for an answer.

A prompt was entered and the Auto Pilot explained that the port was in northern California and that it was Incandium's former headquarters.

The last command that concerned the three at the time was "TAKE-OFF AND LANDING."

"Due to complication of tasks, I will refer you to our submarine manual. There, you will find a comprehensive guide which will instruct you on how to operate the submarine," the Auto Pilot said, before proudly adding, "although *I* can answer many of your questions about the voyage."

A navy-blue hardcover booklet was found lying on the left side of the control board. Ripping through the pages, Jack, Sam, and Mr Berkley found satisfactory explanations and meticulous diagrams. They read all about electricity and fuel and oxygen levels and general maintenance. They were surprised at the simplicity of operation. An important function *even* automated the underway checklist. Pulling a lever, they read, would release low pressure balloons into the water to cause the submarine to rise to the surface in case of an emergency.

The book explained that the submarines had to pass through a large underwater lock-chamber to enter and exit the company's boathouses. (This was the most complicated task.) "One-at-a-time," the book read, "you shall enter the lock-chamber. This is very important to ensure your safety."

Finally looking up from the book, Mr Berkley declared, "I say we go! Taking this submarine to the Sub Port ought to be the best means to stay safe when the storm makes landfall. Anyhow, we need to make sure that the others are ready to leave on this two-day's journey. One submarine won't nearly be enough for *all* the people."

The three went their own ways and searched the

remaining vessels. It was soon found that the four submarines were identical in size and interior design.

By way of the half-turn staircase beneath the chandelier, Jack and Sam discovered an immense cabin. The brothers had discussed whether the submarines would be able to house all of Genoa's people, but, after the exploration, they decided that the intended task *could* be accomplished.

The "merry bunker" was what the cabin was called by the boys. Here, in the merry bunker, a beautifully furnished dining room enveloped the brothers. Encompassing four tables and a bar, the area was filled with gleaming reds and greens. The tables were marble, the floor was covered in velvet-red carpet, and the chairs were strangely shaped. Most of the drinks had been removed from the tiled bar. A chandelier much larger than the others flamboyantly glowed above the Wesleys' heads. Glass portholes could allow passengers to view the underwater depths while eating.

Past the dining room was a kitchen and a hallway. The kitchen was small, but functional. Some canned food was found in its cabinets. There was running water and an icebox. The hallway was lined with paintings of snow-capped mountains and grassy fields. Yellow lightbulbs lit the way.

In an understandable rush, Jack and Sam sprinted through the hall to find a snug bedroom. The space mostly consisted of bunks. A large, fuzzy rug covered the whole floor and three rounded tables stood beside the layered beds. Metal doorways led to a deep wardrobe and a bathroom with two showers and a toilet.

The lowest floor in its entirety was, as Jack said, "fully sumptuous."

Although they were low on foodstuffs, all of the submarines had Auto Pilot computers and enough fuel and battery for the journey to the Sub Port.

As the submarines were now ready for departure, the islanders regrouped. They found that, without a map, the boathouse was quite impossible to locate from a distance. Mr Berkley and his apprentices ran about the rainy park, scattering the entire collection of blue lamps throughout the grass to pinpoint the boathouse's secret entrance.

Jack, Sam, and the blue-vested lighthouse man were almost ready to warn their people of the deadly storm which was well on its way.

"Well," said Jack, placing the final lantern in the grass, "it must be getting late now."

"It must, indeed," declared a sweaty and tired Mr Berkley, "but now our people will have a safe place to stay during the hurricane."

To the east, the sky was almost black, and to the west, the red sun cast its dying light on the shores of a gallant Genoa.

Sam looked at his watch and exclaimed, "My word, it's six o'clock! We've got to leave."

A grueling truth now attempted to dishearten the company: they had yet to evacuate the island.

The three hopeful friends collected their belongings and left the short pine tree and the roadster and the cave. Across the overgrown field and through the forest, they bolted into the blustery, approaching night.

Mr Berkley led the way and proclaimed, "To the harbor, we shall go!"

Chapter Five
The Evacuation

The convertible hummed, its imported gasoline running low. As the hurricane's frightening and deliberate characteristics began to display the island's forthcoming doom, Mr Berkley's station wagon sped along a muddy road. The three had decided to stop by their respective homes to gather belongings.

The peninsula cottage was visited first and Mr Berkley soon carried out a small piece of luggage. He seemed grieved to leave his radio and his neat bedroom and his antiques; the house was cold and quiet. It was an old home, possibly Genoa's oldest. Jack watched with compassion as Mr Berkley bid his precious lighthouse farewell, failing at his attempt to blink away the tears in his eyes. The little red car went on.

Mr Berkley escorted the boys to their doorstep after parking by the oak tree. The brothers hastily removed their belongings from their home: changes of clothes, two handmade contraptions, a yo-yo, playing cards, and a small collection of books. Mr Berkley looked around the once-fishing store, collecting the few things his absent friend might have cared about: a few photographs, a small safe of savings (he decided that John must have kept the rest at Incandium), an antique telescope Mr Berkley had given him, and a PhD certificate.

An apple fell from a nearby tree as Jack closed a car door. "That everything?" Mr Berkley asked.

The two stops were quite brief and, as the final orange and purple colors of twilight swirled into a grey and blue vacuum, the convertible soon screeched to a halt on top of a cliff that overlooked the port. Wind glided across the flowery hilltop, precipitously descending into the quiet harbor-town. Raincoats and flashlights were made available.

Mr Berkley buttoned his coat as he spoke. "Now, being the only ones with knowledge of the boathouse and its submarines, we have an immense responsibility, you see. These are our people, and they all deserve to know what's coming. You two will go to the west harbor with Mr Thompson; I will take the east. I trust we will alert every last one of 'em.

"Your message: the storm of the century is upon us. Evacuate *immediately* to Miller's Park. Bring two bags per family and a week's worth of clothes. We will leave from the boathouse at three A.M. Here," he said, giving Sam a piece of paper with the boathouse's coordinates scribbled on it, "give this to anyone who might need it, few know of Miller's Park. At midnight, we will meet back together at the ocean liner station."

The brothers soon traversed along a path towards

golden lights and the hulls of homey boats. Jack was reminded of the ancient story of Noah. "I hope *our* people will believe us." he thought.

A hollow alarm blared high then low as the sleepy harbor-town began to awake.

"A hurricane is coming," the brothers called from the central pier, "you can't stay! Evacuate the bay! Go to Miller's Park!"

A white-haired man from the Texas Gulf peered his head out of a white sailboat and a raggedy vagabond shyly emerged from a dry-docked dinghy.

A fisher from New Mexico zipped up his overcoat, and, charging at the boys, sneered, "A hurricane? Where on earth did you get such a notion?"

Sam stepped back and then answered, "Sir, we received a telegram from a trustworthy source that a hurricane will make landfall on the island tonight."

The fisher's companion said, "A telegram, eh, I would assume we could trust 'um. Unless it came from the govey. They may clear us out to test their atom bombs like they did in the Marshalls."

The first one's eyes widened. "If they do that, I'll be up in arms!" he proclaimed to the audience that had formed on the dock.

While the New Mexican's were still rambling, a stalky man with a cigar in his mouth waddled up and said, "If this storm be so dangerous, why can't I simply jet out on me boat. She's just as fast as any other, I assure you."

Jack looked down at the man and explained, "This hurricane will be far too powerful for any of these boats to withstand. That is why we will escape on submarines."

"Submarines in Genoa?" the man cried in bafflement. With a chuckle, he continued, "I suppose the Martians told you all this?"

"Where is Mr Thompson?" Jack asked, turning to Sam; a commotion was beginning to erupt.

"I know it's hard to believe, ma'am," Sam explained to a woman who stated that bad weather was a normality, "but we are in grave danger!" Pointing to the tide, he said, "*That* is not normal."

Suddenly, Clive Thompson appeared on the docks. The once-mailman had lived on Genoa for a year and was a respectable man in many ways. He wore a tight blue jacket and a white sailor hat. "Quite a night we have ahead, aye?" he asked, holding a flashlight and pointing it at the two brothers. They nodded silently in response.

Mr Thompson helped the brothers' situation tremendously. Boat to boat and house to house, their message was delivered. Coordinates were copied and explanations were presented. "Yes, submarines." "It's hard to say; it must be a sort of underwater laboratory." "You won't make it if you stay." "Two luggage bags, two luggage bags only!"

While roaming the docks, Jack sighted his friend coming out of his family's boat. "Chad!" he called.

"Evening, Jack," the husky boy shouted, "what's the matter with all the people?"

"A hurricane is on its way," Jack declared, "and you need to get to Miller's park right away."

"Far out." Chad muttered, sighting the bustling townspeople. "I heard that siren and I wasn't sure what was going on."

Chad's father came out in a red and black sweater. He sighed heavily and then impatiently asked, "Could you tell me what's happened, son?"

"Sir," greeted Jack, "we have received a message from Captain Edwards that a hurricane is very close to Genoa. Soon, we will be leaving from Miller's Park."

Chad's father obviously needed more convincing; he had developed a distrust in children, especially the ones that had spent their days in tree houses and at faraway beaches.

Mr Thompson came from behind Jack and said, "Mr Wellington, get to Miller's Park right away. Look here." He pointed at a small map with a mark on it and said, "There's a hidden entrance in the cave here. This is where you need to go to stay safe."

The mustached man nodded slowly and then reluctantly jogged about his boat, calling for his wife.

Mr Thompson told Jack that he would alert the people at the town bar.

Sam's collection of cave-exploring underlings was seen running about the pier, (the teenagers were feverish about the evacuation).

"Mates!" Sam yelled out.

One from the group, Kenny, inquired, "Sam? It true? They're sayin' we're voyaging on sub-aquatic boats." The club of fellow adventure-seekers stood in a huddle, wet from rain and seeking confirmation.

"Righto," answered Sam, bringing about a gasp from the audience, "this is something like the time we were stranded at Flint's Reef when the tide came in—but *this* time, if we stay, we will be killed." Confused silence ensued. "Do you all know where to go?"

"Miller's, right?" asked a freckled boy named Roger.

"Precisely, and be there by three o' clock. Bring a week's worth of clothes, your knives, and some games in case you get bored," Sam explained, "can I trust you all to get there on time?"

Some nodded and a boy named Jet said he would carry on the message. Sam distributed coordinates to his friends, describing to them the cave.

"Well, go flat out, all of you," he instructed, "get to Miller's Park as soon as you can."

A few boys were soon heard relating their anguish about leaving behind their tree forts and all they contained: metal fishing rods and birding books and maps with drawings. A deeper anguish came upon the captains: their precious boats would be given to the storm and its unforeseen powers of destruction.

Jack had a new adventure before him. Would he finally see mountains and prairies? Certainly not beneath the ocean. Who could know what dark things concealed themselves beneath the waves, waiting for victims, for fate?

Crowds of people were now leaving the fishing town. Puddles splashed under the purple light of thunderclouds as families wandered towards the forbidden shore. Occasional automobiles rumbled along muddy roads and over fallen trees.

When he came to the last dock, Jack spotted Lucy. This charming girl had moved to Genoa earlier that winter. She was, what some would have called, a subterranean, collecting her own kind of company wherever she went. Although his friends would have claimed it was one of his reoccurring infatuations, Jack had taken a serious liking to her. "Hey there, Lucy!" he called. The blonde-haired, green-eyed girl was on the deck of her father's longboat and hadn't heard Jack's call, so he shouted her name a little louder.

"Jack," she responded with a gasp, "Jack, what's happening? Everyone's cranked."

"There's a hurricane coming. You have to leave."

Lucy stared at the boy for a moment. "Goodness." she finally muttered, slowly looking towards the sky.

Jack looked towards the sky as well; a belted king-fisher floated beneath a bleak and cloudy firmament.

Lucy asked, "Where will we go?"

"Miller's Park." Jack responded. "You don't know where that is, do you?" She shook her head. "Take this," he said, giving her a piece of paper with the cave's coordinates on it, "when you get to the forest, you need to follow the blue lamps until you arrive at the cave. You will find a door deep inside which will lead you to a boathouse. Bring no more than two bags and make sure you are there before three o'clock."

"I don't understand," she said, "will we stay at this boathouse?"

"No. We will leave from the boathouse to the Sub Port." he stated, only adding to Lucy's confusion. "It's where my father works and it's the only safe place we can stay during the storm."

"Oh." Lucy responded, nodding.

"We'll be traveling inside submarines," described the boy, "there are huge chandeliers and computers that can talk and–" Jack stopped; he realized that he was making a fool of himself. "Anyway, it's quite somethin'."

Lucy smiled and then, with a more serious expression, said, "I'll go and tell my papa right now. I will see you there."

"I hope so!" the boy shouted.

Rain was battering the creaky docks when the Wesleys found each other.

"We've done our part," Sam declared, "let's get to the ocean liner station."

The two rushed across flooded patches of grass and over fallen branches. They stopped to visit the hillside homes, ensuring that *everyone* knew of what was to come.

It was just past midnight when the brothers sat down on an old bench at the island's ocean liner station. A lamp hung over their heads, its flame flickering erratically. The siren wailed without ceasing.

"Where is he? You said he'd be here by now." Jack impatiently recalled once the two had waited for a few minutes. A fresh breeze rushed over a fog-stricken sea and Mr Berkley was nowhere to be seen. Raindrops plummeted upon the harbor with frigid blasts, like miniature bombs in an air raid.

"Just wait a little longer," Sam said, "he's bound to show soon."

Jack stood up and rested against a railing beside the churning water. He wasn't sure what to think. He wanted to see his father, but was afraid that he and his friends wouldn't be welcomed at Incandium. What troubled him was the way his father had spoken to him on certain occasions, as if something evil prowled in the laboratory's shadows.

"Ah," Sam said, standing up and sticking his hands into his coat pockets, "forget waiting—let's go and look for him at the east harbor."

The old lamp flickered more erratically and the cool breeze rushed with less patience. Soon, they were off.

The east harbor was the newer of the two. The docks hadn't any gaps like the ones at the east harbor. The boats were newer and longer. Many families were seen, conversing, packing, preparing. The two brothers crossed the docks in search of Genoa's lighthouse man. Soon, they came upon the *Marine Expedition* where a crowd of men stood at the bow.

"Mr Berkley!" Sam called into the crowd.

"Sam," was the returning shout, "help catch this load!"

The brothers found the lighthouse man leaning over the rail with a group of men at his sides. The green vessel belonged to the town's current supplier of shipping goods, Captain Earnest. Apparently, Mr

Berkley had convinced him to help with the evacuation; food and supplies were being gathered hastily.

"Get this package onto the dock!" Mr Berkley commanded.

"Yes sir." Sam replied, before buckling under the immense weight of potatoes and bags of flour.

Sam and Mr Berkley waved goodbye to Earnest as he left in a loaded truck. The two then fetched Jack from a nearby bench.

Mr Berkley explained, "By now, we must have warned everyone in this blasted port. Let's leave now, we still have much to do."

A rockslide suddenly sent a flood of debris down the harbor-side hill. Jack watched as a rolling oak stump knocked a man off the dock.

"Look!" screamed Mr Berkley, pointing towards the rockslide.

Jack sprinted to the water's edge and saw that the elder was struggling to stay afloat. "I'm coming!" he yelled, diving in. He had forgotten how cold the water would be; it stole the breath from his lungs. He swam frantically towards the sinking man. Diving down, Jack grabbed ahold of a bony hand and pulled the man to the surface.

Once close enough, Sam and Mr Berkley reached down from the dock and lifted the grey-haired man from the water. "Are you okay?" Sam asked.

"I am alright." he replied, coughing all the while.

Jack climbed back onto the dock, shivering.

"Let's give them our coats." Mr Berkley told Sam, before carefully wrapping the two with drier clothing.

Jack recognized the man; he worked at the grocery stand and went by Pete.

"You coming to Miller's Park tonight?" Mr Berkley asked Pete.

"I planned to," the grocer stated, "but I've got a bad leg. And now this!"

"Would you like to come with us in my car?"

"Oh, yes, that would be splendid. And, thank you, young man," Pete said, patting Jack's shoulder, "you are–*very* brave." The grocer exhibited a wrinkly, tenderhearted smile as he spoke.

Though Jack was terribly cold, he was pleased to have helped.

A few minutes later, Jack, Sam, Mr Berkley, and Pete arrived at the car. They soon traversed Genoa's country in the darkness of a stormy night. The downpour gave Mr Berkley a difficult drive; half-way though, the party nearly crashed into a wandering dog.

Many cars were parked beside the forest at Miller's Park. After unloading their luggage, the four detoured around the trail and then darted across the grassy open. The magical lamps illuminated the scene as distraught travelers sought shelter.

Although the boathouse door was left open and there were handy signals to guide the way, some of the islanders had lost their way in the field. While Mr Berkley took Pete inside, the Wesley brothers went out to redirect the people.

Jack was impressed by the evacuation group as he entered back into the submarine house. Many there were conversing about the apparent hurricane and how devastating it would be for anyone left behind. All of the guests were amazed at the eerie, red vessels.

Once he had found the chance, Mr Berkley went to greet his people. Standing on a wooden crate beside the S.A.P., he began to speak. "Hello, everyone!" The people quieted as he continued, "I must apologize for our haste. These lads and I did our best to prepare for departure." Mr Berkley paused a moment; he appeared somewhat nervous before the crowd of fishers, sailors, and vagabonds. "Yesterday, I received a telegram from Captain Edwards, the ocean liner captain. He alerted me about a terrible storm—possibly the worst storm Genoa will have ever witnessed. Fortunately, a friend has given us permission to stay at a science laboratory, a place called the Sub Port. The shelter is surely safe and will protect us from this storm which is now ever so close." Turning to the vessels, he said, "This morning, we will use these four submarines to travel to this Sub Port." The people murmured and the lighthouse man shouted, "Please, don't be alarmed! These vessels are very comfortable and are designed to navigate *themselves* using technology."

A squeaky voice shouted out, "Mr Berkley! With all due respect, have you any experience with operating these vessels?"

The answer to the man's question frightened the exhausted Mr Berkley. "Well, no—not exactly," he replied, "you see, I have never actually ridden in a submarine before."

Although the crowd erupted at this answer, Mr Berkley remained confident in his plan and thundered back, "Despite everything, I ask for your faith in me. I can assure you that this is the *only* way we can save ourselves." The shouting soon faded, and Mr Berkley explained, "We will split into groups and begin the departure soon. I will need three of the most able people to operate the Auto Pilot systems. The travel will last, at most, three days, and there will be enough food onboard to last. You can see me for any questions."

As Mr Berkley stepped from the crate, a number of the people enclosed him. Their questions mostly pertained to the Auto Pilot, voyage procedures, and the Sub Port. Mr Berkley did not have answers to some of the questions, and a few individuals were understandably angered. Poor Mr Berkley was doing the best that he could.

Jack and Sam turned on the submarines' electricity and helped sort their fellow islanders into groups. Their hardest task was to explain to the travelers that pets were not allowed onboard the submersibles. Any dogs would shelter inside the boathouse, a relatively pleasant place for the islander's tail-wagging friends.

Mr Berkley collected the piloting volunteers and brought them into a submarine's control room. He told them of the lime-colored pamphlet and of the navy-blue hardcover. He also introduced them to the speaking computer, demonstrating how to use it.

Eager to show his friend the speaking computer as

well, Jack brought Chad inside after Mr Berkley's lecture.

"It can talk?" the boy remarked in disbelief, itching his head and grinning at Jack.

Jack then led him into the bunker.

"This is unreal," Chad exclaimed, "I've never seen a more fantastic room in all my life."

As they toured the bedroom, Mr Berkley's voice was faintly heard: "Where are you? Jack!"

Jack and Chad soon popped out of the hatch. Coming out, the boys discovered that a submarine had already left.

Seeming quite agitated, Mr Berkley said, "Jack, you! Help us out."

Sam had been working hard, transporting provisions into the remaining submarines; he seemed annoyed that Jack had skipped out on the work.

Seeing that Chad's parents had been anxiously waiting for their son, Jack united the Wellingtons and then showed them to their submarine. While saying goodbye, Jack was relieved to see Lucy and her father in the living room. She waved at Jack and he waved back, beaming.

The second submarine then plunged beneath the water.

"She was just here." a lady told Mr Berkley, when she discovered that her daughter had just gone missing.

"We will look for her, but the submarine will leave without you if you can't find her in time." Mr Berkley stated, hiding his compassion the best he could.

Jack and Sam were sent. They ran about in the rain and soon found a crying girl under a pink umbrella, wandering amidst the lanterns. So, the lady and her daughter were reunited just in time for the departure of the third submarine. You can only imagine how tired the Wesleys were by the end of the sorting and sending off.

Pete the grocer boarded the final submarine along with the Thompsons, a charming family whose father we have already met.

The boathouse was now somewhat quiet aside from the far-off sound of the wind and the rain. All was going as planned.

"Jack. Sam," Mr Berkley called, pointing at his wristwatch, "get your belongings, and one of you, close that door."

Jack ran outside, seeking a proper farewell with Genoa. The trees of the forest were crashing in the distance. His jacket fluttered uncontrollably in the brutal wind, and he leaned forward so that he wouldn't fall back. Although it was very dark and the rain was difficult to see through, Jack sighted a large swell approaching from the sea. He sprinted into the boathouse, closing the door behind him. "Mr Berkley! A surge is about to hit. We need to get underwater, now!"

The lighthouse man was helping carry Sam's second duffle across the dock. "Oh my!" he exclaimed, running past several barking dogs.

Mr Berkley hurriedly followed Jack down the sail ladder. Once the metal hatch was shut, the two scuttled with their luggage past the living quarter and into the control room. Pete and the Thompson family left to the lowest floor to brace for impact.

Mr Berkley and the Wesleys sat in front of the control panel. The automated instructions were helpfully concise, and, soon enough, the fourth and final submarine sunk swiftly beneath the surface. The water outside the control room changed from dark-green to black. Once the vessel had gone deep enough, the Auto Pilot maneuvered the craft towards the ocean.

"To enter the lock-chamber, pull the green lever located below the desk." the Auto Pilot instructed. Mr Berkley immediately yanked the green bar and a circular metal door in the underwater wall of the boathouse began opening mechanically. The submarine ventured through and then the door closed behind.

"Mr Berkley, I think the surge might have already hit." Jack warned fearfully.

"We're leaving either way, my lad." the lighthouse man whispered as he uneasily followed the next instruction. He typed "COMMENCE VOYAGE", pressed the "Execute" button, and then yelled, "Brace yourselves!"

Jack heard Mr Berkley say, "God be with us," as the chamber door opened.

Chapter Six
The Undersea Journey

Orange lights were flashing when he opened his eyes.

"He's awake!" cried Sam.

"What happened?" Jack asked, finding himself on the hard floor of the control room.

The lighthouse man swiftly spun in his swivel chair and said, "You forgot to buckle in—that's what happened!" He spun back.

Sam explained, "The surge whipped the sub and you smashed into the wall. I think you hit this coat hanger."

Jack's head throbbed as his brother helped him off the floor. Headlights cast silver beams on cloudy and swirling water. "Fifty meters deep." the Auto Pilot reported.

"Genoa must be done for after that wave hit." Sam remarked. "Mr Berkley, is the submarine operating properly?"

The man nodded and said, "To my knowledge."

"Can I help with anything, Mr Berkley?" Jack asked, carefully rubbing the back of his head.

"No, you ought to rest. Sam, *you* can stay here

with me."

Jack's stomach was twisted like the staircase. "Everyone in good shape down here?" he asked, walking into the bedroom of the bunker.

Pete nodded and the Thompson children gave cheers from their beds.

Jack climbed a ladder and crawled under heavy sheets. Only now, with the evacuation completed, did he begin to truly realize the fate of Genoa. He wistfully touched the porthole beside him; the glass was cold and wet. Vivid memories violently rushed into the boy's weary mind—memories of a windswept hillside where he and Sam would hide from Mr Berkley for a good laugh, of a treehouse and the customary meetings that were held there, and of his humble home of wood.

A small stream of tears trickled down his tired face as the room's lights were turned off. Sleep came quarter after four.

☾

A pleasant whiff of something familiar lured Jack out of bed. Although the sun had risen hours before, the room was as black as deep space; sunlight was unable to venture as far as the submarine had. After finding the other beds empty, he turned on a lamp.

Jack took a shower and put on some fresh clothes. He was delighted by the hot water onboard. (Genoa's nicest showers were only lukewarm.)

The Thompson family was found eating breakfast

with Pete and Sam in the dining room.

"Look who's finally up," Mr Thompson said with an affectionate smile, setting down a strange-looking glass bottle, "we heard about your nasty fall. How's your head feeling?" "Can Jane fix you some biscuits?" he asked.

Jack said, "Yes, please," and sat down beside Robert and Charlie, the Thompson children. Their mother, Jane, would make the most wonderful treats for the neighborhood kids of Genoa. Biscuits were Jack's favorite and Jane had snuck some onboard before leaving.

Sam came by, obviously in good spirits. "You know what's neat about being on the last submarine to leave," he asked, pointing to a porthole, "you get quite the view."

While Mrs Thomson prepared him breakfast on the electric stovetop, Jack stared through the window. Beyond a dark and gloomy chasm were three glimmering submarines. The shadowy vessels were following each other in perfect order, like trains on a track. A school of silhouetted fish flitted by outside as grey mountains of water sloshed across the ocean's surface so far away. Looking back at his smiling brother, Jack agreed, "It *is* quite the view."

After a breakfast of buttered biscuits and canned peaches, the area was assessed. The ornate chandelier illuminated the dining room and bar with soft, drifting colors. The submarine itself was extremely quiet. Checking the time, Jack read that it was nearly nine. Apparently, the adults had just left to chat over coffee elsewhere.

Charlie, a blue-eyed and curious little girl, asked, "How are you feeling?"

"I'm alright," he said, looking down at her, "how do you like the submarine?"

"It's sure amazing. I really like all of the shiny decorations." she described, pointing to different pieces of embellishment throughout the room.

Jack said that he enjoyed the decorations as well.

Charlie's eleven-year-old brother Robert, a good-natured boy, came from bussing dishes and said, "Jack, you oughta come and see this topnotch chamber we found."

The Wesley boy followed the Thompsons through a round metal door behind the two-turn staircase. It was a small place—a bit smaller than the control room—and mostly empty. There was a rectangular window there, and the three soon sighted a collection of deep sea jellyfish hovering in the distance.

"That one glows!" Charlie exclaimed.

"*That* one has different colors." Robert said, pointing out a large, blue and red jellyfish dancing in the dark.

Jack thought that this would be a great place to read. Looking beyond the glowing spectacle, Jack noticed a backdrop of entangling greenery, a kelp forest in which slimy creatures found refuge from their predators. He envisioned himself trying to swim down as far as they were—he wouldn't have been able to.

Robert asked Jack if playing a game sounded fun.

He said yes and, after acquiring Sam, the children swapped places with the adults in the upstairs living quarter.

A small box was placed on a metal table as the four huddled around. The game was a murder mystery and one of them had secretly committed the despicable crime. The goal was to narrow down the players until only one remained.

Jack was the popular suspect, but Sam and Robert were unknowing that Charlie, with her unassuming smile, was the true murderer.

As the submarine plunged deeper and deeper, Jack enjoyed himself and noticed that his head was feeling better.

When the game was finished, the four children raced downstairs for lunch.

"I wonder what the Sub Port will be like." thoughtfully declared Charlie from her table.

"So do I," agreed Jack, "I wonder if there will be robots there."

"Ooh, that would be neat!" Robert agreed. Lifting his glass, he said, "Maybe they have robots that will do the dishes for us."

The sound of clattering silverware and children laughing filled the colorful room. One might guess that each child felt quite prestigious dining in such an extravagant place.

The lighthouse man was seen coming down the staircase with Mr Thompson not far behind.

"Hello, chaps," called Sam, "everything going smoothly up there?"

Mr Berkley raised his hands and answered, "Indeed! We should be arriving to the Sub Port Wednesday afternoon, God-willing."

After lunch, the children retired to the bedroom. Sam was reading a book about cave exploring while Jack was reading a poem about a drought.

Suddenly, a loud noise was heard. Jack peered out through the porthole beside him and beheld a massive whale swimming beside the submarine! It sung a long and loud, high-pitched song. "Wow!" he gasped, pressing his face against the window. The whale was dark-blue and its eyes were meek.

Charlie and Robert, who were also in the room, crossed the carpet to view the elegant monster. They were amazed at its size; it was nearly as large as the vessel! The whale came slightly closer before gliding away into the aquatic realm.

The rest of the day was somewhat slow. The kids played card games and studied the books and instruments found onboard. Mr Berkley was busy making rounds to ensure each traveler knew about the vessel's important emergency procedures.

The company onboard came together for dinner that evening. They ate canned soup with bread from California. Mrs Thompson also served cheese that she had brought from her home. They ate well on the submarine; their food was mostly canned, but the icebox kept the perishables cold.

Later, Jack was asked to go upstairs and turn off the lights. He was thinking about this undersea journey. He found himself, once again, fearful about meddling with such a secretive company. Although the outcome of the journey was unknown, it comforted Jack to know that his friend Mr Berkley would be with him. As a squid darted by, he was reminded of a special truth: this was an amazing adventure.

☾

A breakfast of flapjacks and fried eggs was pre-pared the next morning. While all the children were gathered in the miniature kitchen, Pete explained to them that an upstairs storage cabinet had remained unopened. The kids finished their meals quickly and then left to explore.

Soon, there were all kinds of things to look at: Charlie found a map of California, Robert found a working projector, and Sam found a medium-format camera.

Once most of the closet items were uncovered, the four agreed to try out the projector. There was film inside the bulky machine already, so, when Robert pointed it at a living room wall and flipped a switch, the light source brightened and the sixteen-milli-meter film began passing along a rotating petal. The audience sat down in chairs and watched carefully as the film began.

The movie opened with large, white text: "Incandium Introductory Film No. 2, 1937." The words disappeared and a group of men and women replaced them. The intelligent-looking folks stood below a long, arcing structure inside a very white room. A man narrated, "Here at the Sub Port, our unanimous mission is progress. As you may see, we faced many challenges while constructing this marvelous lab." Silver cranes lowered towers into a black ocean as the man explained, "However, these challenges did not halt our progress." A picture was displayed of a tunnel and small triangle-shaped objects within. The narrator continued, "Dr Verne has made remarkable strides by contributing to this era of American technology. And no stride of his is quite like his invention of the Sub-Aquatic Probe, a metal-armored, multi-function robot. This technology was sold to our nation's Navy nine years ago, and we have been informed that these bold machines have performed exceptionally in sub-aquatic warfare. Our company spent several years working with the government, and we are still reaping the profit of the partnership."

The children murmured as the film displayed a young John Wesley standing beneath an S.A.P. robot.

"If you are one of the lucky few that Dr Verne has chosen, prepare to share in the bounty. This bounty comes with a price, of course. All information concerning our designs and our facility locations is entirely confidential. Any colleague to release such information must be prepared to leave the corporation and possibly face charges. As you know, these—charges—are now outside of the government's jurisdiction." the narrator stated sternly as the film displayed an odd illustration of a club and a snake.

"Enjoy your stay at the Sub Port, and remember to try some of our delicious blueberry pie." The children murmured as the projection turned black.

Charlie stated, "Jee wiz, what was a strange moving picture!"

"Your pop must make a lot a' dough." Robert said to Sam. Standing up, he declared, "It's no wonder he doesn't tell ya' anything."

Jack pondered of what kinds of "charges" the narrator was referring to, but the others seemingly disregarded that part of the film.

Sam said, "I guess we finally know what father's been up to, huh Jack?"

"Yeah." answered Jack, finding himself much less satisfied with the discovery than he had imagined he would be.

Mrs Thompson called from the floor below and her children left the room.

"After all these years, I could never have guessed that he's been building robots at the bottom of the sea." Sam admitted, following Robert and Charlie to the lower floor.

Jack lethargically picked up the projector to put it away. When he set it on the closet floor, something caught his attention. Looking down, he found a small leather bag. He opened the red pouch and found a pistol and few rounds of ammunition inside. He noticed that each bullet displayed a small inscription of the letter V. He set the pouch back on the floor and closed the closet.

Although no one else seemed to doubt the laboratory's innocence, Jack believed that there was something frightening quietly lurking beneath Incandium's intrinsic mask. Jack slowly passed by the American flag, stepped through the metal door, and tip-toed beneath a chandelier. Hiding behind a cylindrical tube, he spied into the control room. It was empty.

"Two-hundred meters deep." the Auto Pilot reported.

Jack closed the door and then sat down in a swivel chair. Headlight beams glowed ahead as the lime-colored pamphlet patiently waited beside the board. He checked to see if he was still alone in the blue and green fortress. Opening the book, Jack searched for something—anything that would help confirm his fears. He needed to know.

Reading the list in the back of the pamphlet, he sighted a command in his interest. He found the keyboard and typed "PROHIBITED OBJECTS AT THE SUB PORT."

A buzz was heard, and then the phlegmatic voice stated, "Safety is very important to Incandium. Dr Verne does not allow weapons of any kind. He also asks for abstinence from tobacco and alcohol at the laboratory. On behalf of Dr Verne, I thank you for your cooperation."

Jack leaned towards the flashing buttons. "No weapons, eh?" He thought of the inscriptions. "Verne."

He scanned the list of commands and entered "INFORMATION ON MEMBERS OF INCANDIUM."

"Please type the name of the person whose information you seek." the Auto Pilot requested.

The keyboard pattered as Jack spelled "DR VERNE."

"Lewis Verne grew up as a hardworking farmer in Nevada," the Auto Pilot said, "he graduated from Clifford University in nineteen twenty-nine, receiving a master's degree in architecture. After selling ground-breaking technology to the government, he single-handedly began work on the Sub Port, realizing his place in today's world of technological advancements. Several years later, Dr Verne's company is now one of the world's most productive private science laboratories."

Jack was intrigued, yet unsatisfied. The search continued until something nearly jumped off of a page: "THE WESLEY AND VERNE PROJECT."

He hurriedly typed out the command to find the Auto Pilot respond with, "Please enter the pass-phrase."

Confidential information. This might have been what he was looking for.

"Jack, what are you doing in here?" Mr Berkley asked, walking into the room.

Jack gasped. "I was looking for you." he whispered, guilefully closing the pamphlet.

"Were you using the Auto Pilot?"

The boy sat there silently and then decided to shake his head.

Mr Berkley looked at the boy for a few seconds before asking, "Is there something you want to tell me?"

Thoughts raced through his mind as he turned to the elder. "Yes, sir, I wanted to tell you–that–we found a moving picture about the Sub Port."

Mr Berkley crossed his arms and then said, "Oh. How nice. Did you get to see what the place looks like?"

"Yes, it looked very—clean."

"Now I *know* I will like it there!" the inspector declared, laughing.

Jack ventured to the bedroom when he had the chance, finding the other children on the floor.

"Where were you?" asked Robert when Jack came in.

"I was talking to Mr Berkley." he answered.

"You should know that you're missing out on quite the chess tournament. Did you know there was a chess set on this submarine?"

Jack said, "No," and sat on the carpet.

"Sam's beatin' me pretty good." Charlie told him.

Our fearful friend thought of the film and of the ammunition and of Incandium's mask.

Jack skipped lunch, incapable of relaxing. He went to read in the chamber below the stairs, but he couldn't focus on the words. He paced the small bit of floor there was and then sat on a metal box. Jack knew that telling Mr Berkley about his discoveries was the right thing to do, but he couldn't yet bring himself to do it.

Dinner that night was quieter than the previous. Carrots and beef ambled around bowls of broth. The conversation at the table centered around the wildlife observed in the surrounding waters.

Jack walked back to the bedroom after the meal. Mr Berkley surprised him shortly after. "Some good stew, wouldn't you say?" he asked.

The Wesley boy nodded.

"Something wrong?" the man asked compassionately. "You seemed bothered at the table."

"Not really."

"Homesick, aren't you?"

"You could say so." said Jack. He had a strange feeling that Mr Berkley knew the truth all along. "Actually, I need to tell you something."

The lighthouse man asked, "What is it, my lad?"

"I *was* using the Auto Pilot earlier," Jack confessed, "I discovered a gun onboard, so I asked it some questions."

"You found a gun?" the lighthouse man asked.

Jack nodded.

The man took a step closer and inquired, "Have you told anyone else?"

"No, I haven't."

He asked Jack to show him the finding. After his godfather observed the lustrous handheld, Jack told him, "The Auto Pilot said weapons are contraband."

Mr Berkley explained, "One might find a gun onboard any commercial vessel, my lad. You know that this is most likely just a safety precaution."

The boy pondered the knowledgeable man's assumption and said, "I'm sure that you're right." Jack then shook his fist and whimpered, "I just don't see why father would tell us to come if he might get in deep trouble for it."

The lighthouse man sat beside Jack and said, "We haven't seen your father many times in the last few years, but I know something very important: I know how much he loves you. And even though so much has separated you two, we have reason to trust him. You see, when your father found out that the storm was coming, he probably didn't even consider the consequences, whatever they might be. He thought only of his sons and how badly he wanted to make sure they stay safe."

The boy looked up and asked, "You really think so?"

"I *know* it!"

Jack hugged his friend tightly.

"This is hard on all of us," Mr Berkley explained, "so far we have lived blessed lives. Now, we must face our challenges, the good, and the bad."

Jack looked down and then back to the kind face of the lighthouse man. "Did you know Dr Verne used to be a farmer?" he asked.

Mr Berkley seemed surprised. "Dr Verne seems to me the strangest of these undersea scientists."

They laughed and each went his own way.

Jack fell asleep feeling much less afraid, victorious over his fearful mind.

☾

The next morning, the Sub Port seemed to be the

only thing to talk about.

After putting on some pants and a sweater with a polo neck, Jack sought some breakfast.

In the kitchen, he was greeted by his brother and shown some little pictures of the Sub Port that had been found. Sam explained, "I think that this is their production room. And this—this is where they lodge. This here must be some kind of cafeteria." The pictures interested Jack. The Sub Port looked very spacious and technological.

The Thompson children were restless about arriving at the Sub Port, and their parents had a particularly tough job keeping Charlie in good behavior.

Mr Berkley kept watch from the control room, and the children filtered through constantly.

"Is that it?" Jack asked.

"No, I don't think so." the patient man stated.

"I think I see it!" Robert exclaimed.

"No, that's a volcanic formation."

Jack later packed his belongings in the bedroom, folding his clothes neatly. He happened upon a hardcover journal he had brought on the trip. This was a special journal that had belonged to his mother. He had never written in it, but saved it for a special story. He was considering writing about the whale when he heard someone yell, "We've made it!"

Jack was immediately in the control room, and so were the others. As the submarine tilted downwards, a pen rolled across the control board. The vessel began descending towards a giant, black hole in the reef. It was apparent that the Sub Port lie not on top of the sea floor, but *within*.

"What is that?" Charlie asked, referring to a shifting shadow in the distance.

"I think I've seen that before!" Mr Thompson said, squinting at the darkness.

"It's an S.A.P.!" Sam announced.

A replica of the decommissioned robot at the boathouse roamed the colossal caverns of the surrounding terrain.

"There are others." Mrs Thompson reported, tapping on a porthole.

The multi-legged machine was accompanied by several others, each meticulously and diligently scavenging the depths.

The S.A.P. robots soon stood above the audience as the submarine descended into the frightening cave. The downward motion of the vessel eventually became horizontal once more. The portholes now looked out at tunnel walls where hydrothermal vents became homes for strange, greedy shrimp and red-tipped tube worms seeking warmth in the frigid waters.

"This is one *big* cave." Mr Berkley remarked under his breath. The spectacle caused the once lively chamber to become utterly silent. For the first time in over two days, the submarine began to decelerate.

These people of Genoa now beheld the awaited destination. A superior structure of genius design protruded from the tunnel's ceiling. It was hidden with exceptional skill.

The submarine headlights illuminated the exterior of the laboratory where thick glass separated the formidable ocean water from breathable air.

As the group went deeper into the tunnel, they passed near the Sub Port's perimeter. Looking up, Jack saw that the inside of the Sub Port was perfectly white. He viewed several long desks lining glass walls. Chandeliers like the ones in the submarines hung from the ceiling, and bright-colored furniture embellished certain sections of the establishment.

People wearing lab coats and suits were passing by desks and retrieving things from cabinets. Many came to view the submarines as it passed beneath the establishment. Others were sighted running briskly across the floor.

"This is even more intriguing than what I had imagined!" admitted Pete.

The Thompson children conversed with each other about what they called the "underwater hotel." Mr Berkley waited tensely at the control board in case of any unexpected problems.

There was air above the submarine, in a portion of the floor of the Sub Port, and, as the leading submarines ascended, the folks realized that this sight was an indoor pier. The vessel soon became motionless. Mr Berkley obeyed the Auto Pilot's instructions, and they were soon rising upwardly into a moon pool.

The Auto Pilot docked the submarine perfectly. As was planned, each of the other submarines had already docked in a similar fashion, one-at-a-time and in their respective places.

Jack held his baggage tightly and waited beneath the brass periscope in the sail. He was thinking about his father and the fantastic story he had to tell him.

As the travelers from the island of Genoa collected their things, a strange aura was sensed throughout the submarine.

Mr Berkley hesitantly lead the rest to the hatch. "I suppose we've made it safely at last!" he declared.

But, as you may have feared, safety was far from guaranteed.

Chapter Seven
The Time Vessel

Our story has arrived at the frightening yet equally curious events which took place at the underwater laboratory called the Sub Port.

It was on the fourth of November, in nineteen fifty-one, that the construction of a strange machine was completed—a machine unlike any other created before it. It was called the time vessel, and by its hope were two men consumed. As a Frank Chacksfield hit echoed through a grotto and a calcite ceiling slowly eroded under the weight of five hundred meters of ocean, Dr Lewis Verne and Dr John Wesley celebrated their accomplishment.

"A machine that transcends time!" Dr Verne bellowed, raising his sweaty arms into the air under soft chandelier light.

"So it is." said John, smiling momentarily and then placing his steaming electrode in its place on a welding stand. Marie waited just beyond the metal walls of the time machine.

An orange sun may have been descending over a vast ocean, but the doctors couldn't have known, for they were involved in an obsession. Each had his own reason: one sought power, the other, a lost companion. But both men were deceived.

John was feeling dizzy, and thirsty. "What time is it?" he asked, picking up his half-empty bottle of *Great Basin Beer*.

"About six-thirty." said Dr Verne, glancing at his wristwatch and slipping on his lab coat.

John pointed to a tunnel within the rocky wall of the grotto where a four-wheeled cargo-cart held a stack of aluminum sheets. "Will we need any more material?" he asked.

"Our work here is done!" Dr Verne proclaimed, his black hair gleaming as he roamed the floor. "Only an army could stop us now." He spun around and waved a hand towards the magnificent creation.

Streams of five-inch-wide electron-accelerator tubes crowded the box's alluring exterior. A feat of seemingly pure genius, the time vessel was composed mostly of an exotic compound of a newly discovered metal. The surface of the machine appeared to be of a blue shade from a distance, but was found to be black when observed closely. John thought it to be a thoroughly entrancing spectacle, although it did frighten him. The inside of the machine was uncomfortably tight, the walls being several feet thick and leaving just enough space for a person to recline in a chair. Electrical sparks set the exterior of the machine ablaze during use. Years of testing could only fairly prepare the doctors for time travel. Who could know what it would actually be like for a human to utilize such a terrifying means of transportation?

Beside a long ladder latched onto the northern extremity of the grotto, the two stood, preparing to leave.

"Soon, we will need to stage some electrical diagnostic tests," Dr Verne explained, "as you know, the Sub Port will be quite different until the time vessel is ready."

"I have a request." the engineer called, as his colleague stepped onto the ladder. John stood tall; he could sense a raging battle within his mind. "May I visit Genoa this week? I would like to see my children one last time before we get—"

"You dare leave again!" roared Dr Verne, taken aback. "We finally finish the machine and you want to leave?" Coming unbearably close to the startled engineer, he said, "At one moment, you want nothing of that island—the next, you have the nerve to leave again." The man then covered his face with his palms. Lowering his dirty hands, he sighed. "You know how crucial you are in this project—if one thing goes wrong, you better be here to fix it." Dr Verne stepped up onto the ladder and stated, "You've got five days, Wesley. Get going as soon as possible."

"Thank you," John shouted up the vertical passage, "thank you, Dr Verne. Have yourself a good night."

John knew that the powerful man's record was far from clean. But, circumstances would not allow this fact to become an excuse. After all, the man was a victim of a brain injury; surely, he could not be held fully responsible for his actions. John would continue to lie to himself in order to stay sane as he worked with the notorious genius.

~

It would be the first version of the time vessel capable to transport humans. Requiring megawatts of power to operate, the machine would be fully charged on the seventeenth of December. Dr Verne and Dr Wesley waited in anxious expectation as the time vessel received all of the electrical power that the Sub Port could harness. The two directors would have to fabricate reasons why the facility's submarines have a limited power supply and, therefore, why the workers could not leave. Thus, many would be present for the four weeks preceding the time vessel's maiden voyage.

In the Sub Port's more spacious and evident places, Incandium's twenty-eight employees were working many hours and completing difficult endeavors, unfortunately and unknowingly supporting the megalomaniac's selfish ambitions.

John was unsure exactly what these ambitions were, despite the closeness of his professional relationship with Dr Verne. The Oregonian *had* discovered that his colleague hadn't designed the time machine himself. Someone had actually given him the plans. Regardless of what the president's purposes were and how he came into possession of the time vessel's blueprints, it was clear to John that the blue box of metal was of utmost importance to him.

On the day that John returned from his short trip to Genoa, the white-haired, brown-eyed doctor was certainly disheveled. He had been to Genoa many times over the previous years, but never had he feared his children's safety as sincerely as he did on this occasion. He understood completely the position he put himself in by writing the message and preparing the boathouse, but he also knew what was coming.

~

They took turns watching the time vessel. Golden sparks were flying, bouncing, and dissipating into the air as John sat in a wooden folding-chair. He was thinking about Marie. Her black locks, her crystal eyes. Her imagination, her bravery. The love that he had had for her. The love that he still had for her.

He closed his eyes and dreamt that she stood beside a church pillar in a blue dress. The dress was nearly bluer than the sky behind her. She smiled, then turned. He followed. They ran down the side of a sandy hill and fell beside the foamy waves. He felt her cheek. She smiled, stood up, and skipped around a boulder. "Marie." John called, following her small footprints in the sand.

Suddenly, black clouds descended on the beach, Marie was gone, and children's screams replaced her. "Marie?" the petrified engineer called.

Turning to the ocean, John sighted a group of people running about on a small island. A towering wave was about to sweep over them. The troubled man waded desperately through the water. He needed to get them to safety! "Jack? Sam? Boys!"

"Father!" cried Sam as darkened clouds consumed the dream.

John fell on the floor. The time vessel looked down on him with an electric glare.

This dream had haunted him for weeks now, and for good reason: strange storms brewed over violent seas when the time vessel was turned on, and the storms grew more powerful with each test. With no way to prevent the confounding byproducts from resulting, the doctors were tampering with forces beyond their control. Thus was the misfortunate dilemma and perilous problem by which the poor man suffered for many months.

~

Speak to the employees, take a nap, watch the time vessel. The routines became second-nature to the aging engineer.

An alarm began blaring annoyingly somewhere in the distance. John's heart raced as he pushed his spectacles up his nose. Something was wrong; the alarm hadn't rung in a very long time. He began walking towards the ladder.

Suddenly, a shapeless shadow descended into the room. Dr Verne materialized. "You traitor!" he shouted. A beam of misfortunate light fell upon the president's face. "Four submarines are coming our way and you are the only one I know who could be responsible for this." Grabbing John's collar and pulling him towards his red face, Dr Verne questioned, "You did this, didn't you?"

John's glasses had fallen back down his nose. He nodded.

Dr Verne let go of his colleague's collar, and John nearly fell over. "You pathetic sewer," the president sneered, "I am not ready for this, no, not at all. This is *your* problem now! And if you slow me down by one minute—" He stopped and breathed more slowly.

"I couldn't let them stay, Dr Verne, you know that. This storm is much, much worse than the last one. My sons would have had no chance."

"I thought we had an agreement, Wesley; we were to comply to our rules under *any* circumstance. And how, may I ask, are you going to save your precious Marie if these blokes expose our work?" The strange director looked at John with utter dread.

"They won't, I promise. We'll put on our show— the same way we do when corporate comes." John described, buttoning his lab coat with trembling fingers. He knew he needed a good plan. "I can have Ned get the rooms together."

"Four submarines, Wesley! How many did you invite?"

John closed his eyes as he answered, "I told David Berkley to evacuate the island if he must."

"Blast!"

John retorted, "We have three days—"

"Two-and-a-half." Dr Verne shouted back.

"Right, but we will have plenty of help." Signaling towards the laboratory above, John said, "We've just got to tell them that that we planned this, right?"

The president kicked an empty bottle across the stone floor. Nodding slowly, he walked away. "You are going to pay for this, one way or another."

"You know I'm on your side, Dr Verne." John yelled across the room. But, for the first time in many years, both of them doubted the idea that they *were* on the same side. His head throbbed as he picked up his beer bottle. John smiled to himself; he would see his children again.

Chapter Eight
The Sub Port

Jack stood on the bottom rung of the wooden ladder, waiting impatiently. Soon, Mr Berkley and Mr Thompson were spinning the hatch's silver turn-wheel. With the other children bumping up against him, Jack had trouble seeing the boathouse from inside the submarine sail. Looking out, he found that the walls were white, bare, and towering. Velvet red and teal green were observed in the room's minimal decorations. Bright white fixtures popped out of covert rifts in the high ceiling.

"Come on up! Ladies first!" Mr Berkley hollered from the top of the ladder.

The air felt warm and still when Jack emerged. He climbed down the side of the sail and then joined his friends on the dock. The platform was made of a silky marble, and the walls, something similar. Brass-coated fuel-dispensers were positioned at each dock beside a potted cactus. A short hole was sighted within the far wall; a four-wheeled cargo-cart sat on tracks, waiting outside a mysterious tunnel. On the closer side of the pier, Jack saw a massive wooden door.

The islanders in the other submarines would stay put until Mr Berkley's signal. "Where are the employees?" the lighthouse man asked, buttoning his collar. He nearly jumped when three men busted through the nearby door. As the trio approached, the lighthouse man walked out to greet them.

The man in the center, a purple-coated, green-eyed man, shook the elder's hand and said, "Hello, my name is Ned.

Jack noticed that the man had a long tattoo of Mount Rainier on his left arm.

You are Mr Berkley?"

"Yours truly," he answered, "we have come by permission from Dr John Wesley."

"We've been expecting you." Ned remarked, smiling.

"Have you?" Mr Berkley asked, turning to Jack and Sam who stood behind him on the dock.

"And, how many have you brought with you?" Ned asked, brushing off his dark-purple coat.

After biting his lower lip, the lighthouse man responded, "Sixty-two."

One of the men in the trio wore a surprised face as Ned asked Mr Berkley to bring out the guests. Mr Berkley then turned and signaled with his hands. Without hesitation, the grateful and astounded townspeople from Genoa began gathering on the marble docks.

"Will there be room for them all?" the vested islander inquired, before turning to observe an ornamented pillar beside the dock.

"Uh—assuredly, sir," answered a green-coated man, the one that had looked surprised, "and we express our condolences about what has happened to your island, Mr Berkley."

Pointing with a white finger, Ned said, "Now, gather your friends. We are about to show you around the place."

Once the majority of travelers had exited the submersibles, Mr Berkley bellowed, "Good afternoon, ladies and gentlemen! I trust that you've had safe and enjoyable travels. If you would now please collect your belongings, we are going to follow these men here!"

The crowd cheered and began gradually moving through the boathouse in groups.

Jack was busy keeping watch for his friends. Soon, he heard someone yell his name. Squinting, the boy sighted Lucy running towards him.

She came up, dropped her bags, and hugged the boy. "Oh Jack, wasn't it wonderful," she asked, "it was such an adventure!"

Jack was nodding as she spoke. "It really *was*." he replied. The two looked away from each other and then at each other. "I—like the color of that scarf." Jack said.

Lucy looked down at two dangling strands of pink. "Thank you." she replied, shrugging.

After passing through the towering, wooden doors, the boy and the girl found themselves in a hallway. A long hallway. And Jack thought it strange that he hadn't yet seen his father. Lucy's parents called her over, so the two said goodbye.

Jack's brother took her place soon after. "That man in the purple jacket said that we're headed to the cafeteria." Sam described.

An orange-coated man, the third one in the trio, waited for the people to pass by before shutting the door behind them. He did so with a stern face, expressing a particular annoyance.

There were occasional doors in the hallway, but it seemed to serve primarily as a connection from the boathouse to the rest of the facility. The doors were numbered with little gold inscriptions. Soon, soft music was heard: a jazzy tune like the one played in the submarines.

"This is the cafeteria!" Ned announced as the crowd gathered at another tall, wooden door found at the end of the hall.

The following room was built in the shape of a circle. It had a domed, expansive ceiling and an intricate water fountain in the center. Certain parts of the floor were made of thick glass. Stone walls were coated with a shiny finish and the jagged reef poked out in random places. The area was void of people, for it was about three in the afternoon.

"Dr Verne likes us to gather together for our meals," Ned explained, "so he built the cafeteria in this dome because it was the largest space provided inside of this underwater tunnel." The man pointed at the jagged reef. "Dr Verne also likes to remind us where we are, lest we forget, so he allowed the reef to protrude through the building envelope. The reef's protrusion actually makes the building stronger." He said this, nodding with pride.

Jack spotted Chad wandering in the midst of the group, so he ran to greet him. "Chad, Chad!" he called.

"Jee wiz, Jack," his friend exclaimed, "things just keep getting better and better, don't they?"

"This place is so enormous." Jack declared, motioning to the overwhelming surrounding.

Chad stated, "I'm getting the feeling we haven't seen half of it." "Where's your pop?"

"I'm not sure," Jack admitted, "but I think we should see him soon. Once the tour is over, maybe."

"Here's our kitchen." Ned declared, stopping at the edge of the cafeteria where a long, white arc stretched over red and white tiles. The cafeteria wall opened into a far-reaching kitchen where metal arms twirled. "Our machinery does most of the work over here," Ned explained, "see, this machine is doing the dishes for us." The tour guide stepped away as children rushed to the counter where a pair of multi-jointed arms lowered and raised dishes and silverware. "When it's mealtime, you can choose from the menu by ordering on the electronic counter here." Ned placed his hand on an illuminating screen near the kitchen's perimeter. The place smelled of seafood and fresh produce; how the vegetables and fruits could be so fresh Jack did not understand. What looked like a part of the kitchen began gliding around at the other side of the kitchen. "And *that* is one of the many appliances that Dr Verne has invented," Ned asserted, "it's part sink, part oven, part refrigerator, and part toaster. It's also mobile, as you can see." This sparked a laugh from a few bewildered individuals who would have never dreamt of such a creation.

While Ned was speaking, Jack perceived the sound of footsteps and turned to see a man in a black suit running in the distance. The man looked at Jack and then turned away. "Hey." Jack whispered, hitting Chad. But, when the boy looked, the man was gone. "Never mind." grumbled Jack.

"Lastly, the cafeteria restroom is just beyond the kitchen over there." Ned stated, turning on his heels. "This eating area will only be available to you at mealtimes, but you can find snacks in your housings. Let's move on to the research-center. I am permitted to show you a *few* of our projects. When we finish up there, you will have a chance to meet our president."

The people followed Incandium's representative trio to the other side of the cafeteria and through a final wooden door. There was a short hallway here, before a metal door with a pass-code lock on it. The orange-coated fellow typed in a code and covered the lock with his free hand. The door swung open and a rushing wave of sundry noises was heard. "Welcome to the research center!" Ned yelled.

Groups of men and women walked about the room. Others huddled around tables. Several S.A.P. limbs hung from a vaulted ceiling, and small, moving parts dotted the room like shells on a beach. The room's walls were made completely of glass, and the end of the laboratory was rounded off. Green and red lanterns illuminated people's desks in the distance. Most of the loud noises dissipated as the visitors flooded in.

"Everyone, welcome our guests!" Ned commanded, before the employees waved somewhat reluctantly in response. "These are the people whose island was struck by that *terrible* storm," the purple-coated guide recounted, "we are pleased to have them stay with us for the time being."

The group followed Ned, who smiled to himself and remained mostly quiet. Desks lined the perimeter. Couches and tables were placed in empty patches. Radios crackled and produced pleasant melodies. The guide cut short, circling around the closer half of the room and avoiding much of the laboratory's equipment and workers.

Jack was bewildered by what he saw. A pungent, metallic smell jumped from a quickly rotating machine by a green wall. Blue and purple light sparked from a round instrument that moved back and forth on the nearby floor. The colors were bright and magical.

A man in a white lab coat said, "Have a gander," and put a smooth and cold object in Jack's hand. It was immobile at first, then began hovering above Jack's palm.

"What a charge!" said the Wesley boy, gasping.

"Now, put your hand upside-down." the man excitedly directed.

Jack slowly rotated his hand, and found that the metal orb remained fixed beside his palm, then hung like a pendulum would from an invisible string. The man took the shiny object back, without explaining to Jack and the surrounding spectators the purpose of the tiny, floating invention.

Jack joined Chad and Lucy, and they stopped at the S.A.P. arms which hung from the ceiling.

"Don't touch these!" an African-American woman exclaimed when the children reached out to examine the metal limbs. "These are–very expensive," she said before softly laughing, "would you like to see what they can do?" The children nodded and the woman reached into her lab coat and produced a silver object from one of its pockets. Inserting the key into a nearby computer of sorts, she started the robotic arms. One rotated about, reached down, and picked up a fork. The exterior of another shuffled about and extracted a rectangular device from inside itself. It was a lighter, and the children stepped back when a yellow flame appeared quite suddenly. Before they could watch the rest of the S.A.P. performance, the woman said, "Get going now, your party is leavin' y'all behind!"

Turning, Jack saw that his brother was waving at him from the entrance of the room; sadly, they had to skip the rest of the laboratory tour. Jack, Chad, and Lucy left the bustling laboratory and the orange-coated fellow swiftly closed the metal door behind them.

Taking a left turn, they found themselves in a lobby. The room was shadowy near its extremity, but well-lit in the center, as though a spotlight hung above the bustling crowd. Exploding with an aroma of bleach and other disinfectants, the black, marble floor was utterly clean and acutely slippery. Mr Berkley almost took a fall and glanced around to see if anyone had noticed.

Everyone seemed to be waiting for someone, or something. Between two cacti, Ned stood, smiling. Jack was sure he could see a stream of elevators in the dark room behind the purple-coated man. "Any minute now." he stated. He viewed his wristwatch, looked around, and then declared, "There he is!"

A man in a sleek, black suit jogged out from shadows, firmly shook Ned's hand, and then turned to the people. "Oh my," he cried in a roaring voice, "would ya' look at all these lovely people!" A fisherman tilted his head; he was surely puzzled. "This, as you now know, is the Sub Port and the headquarters of Incandium Science Labs. I am the president of the company and it's my pleasure to be hosting you." The man had black hair, brownish-green eyes, and a light-brown face. He was very tall. "We do not typically host like this, so I apologize for any inconveniences you might experience during your stay." Dr Verne's roaming gaze halted at Mr Berkley, and Jack perceived something markedly dark in the president's eyes for just a moment. "We are about to show you to your lodgings," the man said, "but first, a word from your neighbor, and my colleague, Dr Wesley."

Jack and Sam found each other and rushed towards the front of the crowd. They watched as their father stepped into the light.

"Hello everyone. My name is John Wesley." the engineer said. His face was tired, and his voice, weak. He searched the crowd as he spoke. "Some of you may know me, I used to live on Genoa. My children still live there, Jack and Sam, they are—" John paused when he saw them. He smiled at their beaming faces, forgetting where he was. "Oh," he said, when Dr Verne whispered in his ear, "I am *so* glad to know that you are all here. I hope your journey was comfortable and that there were no mishaps along the way. Now, I can assure you that you will enjoy being here at the Sub Port—it is—an accommodating place."

Ned proceeded by guiding the islanders to the elevators, while John navigated the crowd to find his children.

"Jack, Sam." he whispered as tears filled his eyes. He hugged each boy. "I was so scared for you two."

"You'd never believe what we went through to get here," Jack declared, "this has been our greatest adventure yet."

John sighted Mr Berkley nodding in agreement behind his children. "Thank you, David, thank you so much." the engineer said, walking to and hugging his friend.

The lighthouse man, in return, recounted, "It was *your* message that brought us here."

"How have you been?" Sam asked.

"I've been just fine, Sam." John said, nodding.

Jack, Sam, their father, and Mr Berkley were entering into the shadowy room. The shadows were soon replaced by dim, red lights, and the people eagerly waited to leave the hot room and to get to their lodgings.

Mr Thompson found John and talked to him for a short while, thanking him and asking some questions. John talked to several other islanders and then came back to his children.

"Father, why is it so hot in here," Jack asked, "can they not afford air conditioning?"

"We are doing surveys on the electric systems here," John hesitantly replied, "so we have to cut down on how much electricity we use."

Jack said, "Oh," and his white-haired father thought of the time vessel. By now, Dr Verne was probably already back in the grotto, drinking and pacing erratically.

"Well, I just hope our rooms are cooler than this." Mr Berkley said, wiping his forehead with a light-blue handkerchief he seldom used.

Ned came out of what seemed to be a closet and announced, "I can take you to your rooms now! Please separate into groups of about twelve. We have three rooms a floor, and five available floors. It'll be a tight fit, but surely not as tight as those submarines you've been on." He said the last bit laughing. (He was a becoming a sweaty mess like the rest.)

The four walked into an elevator.

"Which floor are *we* staying on?" Mr Berkley asked, observing red wallpaper portraying gold flowers.

John pointed a finger at an illuminated button on the elevator wall. "Three." he answered.

Ned's friends led various groups into the rooms. Jack thought the place seemed just like a hotel. Stepping out of the elevator, he found bright blue carpets about the floor, white walls surrounding, and peculiar paintings scattered about the walls. Chad waved from down the hall, stepping into a room under the command of his comical parents–his father wore a top hat and the mother was carrying a cane though she hadn't any use for it.

Jack asked his father whether he could stay with their party and talk. Then, John grouped the three into a circle and said, "I am sorry to say that my work is going to keep me very busy while you're here. I actually have to get going now." He lifted a shaking wrist and observed two tiny brass arms of supreme power.

"John," said Mr Berkley, "before you leave, please take this." He lifted one of the two luggage bags he carried. "Inside are some of your belongings from home. I thought you'd want to make sure they stay safe." The lighthouse man also offered his friend a compassionate smile, one that broke through secrets and lies.

John took the bag and thanked Mr Berkley. He wondered what was inside, for he had assumed that everything he needed was with him at the Sub Port.

"Well, I hope you enjoy your room." was his remark. "See you three tomorrow."

Jack was undeniably frustrated and Sam seemed at least bitter. "Bye father." they chimed, with whatever gaiety they could muster.

"Goodnight, my friend." the lighthouse man said.

The orange-coated man watched from the end of the hall as the three refugees went into their room and John revisited the elevators.

Jack threw his baggage on a bed with black sheets. Boxes of orange and white jumpsuits were found in the closet. Hung from a metal rod were two sets of scuba gear. The far wall was composed of coral reef and fish swam in a box of glass. When Mr Berkley turned on the lamps, the reef wall was illuminated, but the fish went unidentified; they were red with large scales and larger eyes.

"Nice place." Mr Berkley said, sitting on a bed.

A small ice box in the closet held cookies, crackers, cans of soup, and milk. A stove was found beside the kitchen sink. Once Mr Berkley flipped various switches, an air conditioning system began cooling the stuffy lodge.

Jack placed his clothes in some wooden drawers beside a bed. Even if they weren't to stay long, he wanted to settle in. He folded his clothes nicely and organized them by type.

There were two twin-sized beds in the room, and Sam had already taken one. Mr Berkley would take the other, of course, so Jack would sleep on the floor. It was a comfy carpeted floor, though, and Jack fell asleep quickly.

•

Dr Wesley and Dr Verne convened that night in Dr Verne's elegant lounge. The two were leaning against a white wall in the empty room. Orchestral tunes were marching from a radio and grey puffs of smoke clouded the atmosphere as the two bickered. The Sub Port was suddenly a busy place; plans needed to be decided upon, and it was not long before the doctors were furiously debating about their options.

"So, this is the way things will be now?" the president questioned in a belligerent manner.

John was sweating and aching. He felt sick, like chemicals were sloshing around in his stomach. Wasn't this the best he could do? But, angered fishermen and sailors *would* be throwing their fists and cursing the company soon enough. "I trust that they will be satisfied," he comforted, "we'll let them into the cafe three times a day and give them the best we have until we can power up the submarines again."

"Giving them the best we have is a challenge in itself," Dr Verne explained, digging his cigar into a small heap of ash, "but don't you forget that we must also keep this island folk out of our business." Dr Verne laughed to himself as he poured a strong drink at his long, black countertop. "It's funny, no, it's strange. I just don't understand how all this happened now. I would have allowed these island-folk to have come any other blasted year, or even month."

John was shaking his head. (He refused to believe in such a thing as fate.) "It's our fault they came. We created the storm that brought them here."

"That's not true!" exclaimed Dr Verne, before downing his drink. "*You* invited them."

"I had to!" he cried.

Beneath electric light, Dr Verne roamed towards his bed-chamber. "It's time for your shift. I need some sleep."

John did too, and maybe even more so. But, he didn't say so; for, he would never ask much from the one who fed him, who could make his dream come true.

After descending into the grotto, John fell into a green folding-chair. The time vessel sat there, slurping electrons, power. "Please, please work." John whimpered. Sleep came much later.

☾

Innumerable photons penetrated Jack's eyelids as the smell of coffee filled his lungs. "Mr Berkley?" he asked.

"Good morning, my lad." a lively and affectionate man said, looking down with a steaming cup in his right hand.

Jack closed his eyes and pensively frowned. "I had a nightmare." he stated.

"What was it about?" the lighthouse man inquired.

Jack propped himself on a nearby bench. "You and Sam were with me in the boathouse here," he explained, "I don't know why, but we were in a hurry to leave. We were coming to a submarine and about to go inside. All of a sudden, Dr Verne came at us. He pulled out a handgun and shot me in the chest! I fell to my knees, gasping." Sam was now listening, seemingly intrigued by the vision. "I called for you two, but you boarded the submarine without me. As I lay there, the lights went out and the room began flooding with water. I couldn't breathe, and—I must have died."

Mr Berkley put an arm around the boy.

"It was just a dream." said Jack.

"My lad, I would *never* leave you behind. You know that." Mr Berkley comforted, looking up into a yellow bulb in the ceiling. "I will protect you with all my ability. Understand?" He smiled and Jack nodded, smiling as well.

"I don't know what got into me." the boy said, rubbing his face and getting off the bench. "Any coffee left?"

Sam raised a mug of black drink and replied, "It's much better than Genoa's."

Jack asked, "Have you two left the room yet?"

Sam was shaking his head as the lighthouse man explained, "They've locked the doors, Jack. But, we were told that we can come out for breakfast at eight."

"Why would they do that?" Jack questioned.

"They've been kind enough to give us a place to

stay and food to eat. We can't ask for much more."

Jack put on some clothes, checked the time, and watched the fish. Sam explained that he had heard some loud noises in the night; he wasn't sure what had made the noise, but he said that it was like banging metal.

At exactly eight o'clock, the lodging's door unlocked. The three islanders stood behind the exit, preparing to leave.

"Almost forgot! My shoelace." Jack bent down and tied his right shoe. They were then on their way.

Gerald, a Texan acquaintance, joined the three in an elevator and Mr Berkley asked him how his night was.

"I can't complain," the brawny traveler answered, "my pal Christopher had to sleep on the floor, though. Almost tried fishing in that tank in our room." Gerald chuckled. "Chris said 'em fish were fit to eat."

From a cone-shaped intercom, a trumpet arduously climbed high up the treble scales. The elevator door opened. "Thank you again, Mr Berkley. The way the storm looked when we left, I don't care where we're stayin'. Heaven must've sent you, I know it!" Walking away, the man cheered, "Have a good day!"

Mr Berkley might have been blushing when his apprentices looked at him. A trail of hungry people followed an inviting breakfast waft through the wooden cafeteria doors.

A man in a white lab coat passed by the three as they crossed through the dome. The well-dressed employees clearly stood out from the islanders; some sat at tables in groups, others were leaving for work. Jack saw that they couldn't help but show their disgust in the island folk; it was as though simple peasants had just infiltrated a band of dignified knights. But, the monarch confusingly commanded the knights not to attack, but to share their castle and privileges.

After a failed attempt at utilizing the illuminating screen in the kitchen, spinning arms of metal yielded the best-tasting omelet Jack had tasted in a long time. Sam received flapjacks, and Mr Berkley went for some French toast with walnut crust.

To their surprise, Jack, Sam, and Mr Berkley were invited by a man named Chuck to eat at his table. "So, you are the chap that brought all the people, aren't ya'?" the red-haired fellow demanded.

Mr Berkley wetted his lips and sat down. "I suppose I am. But, I was–we were invited."

The slender man laughed. "I know you were. I'm not cross! We are pleased to have ya'. I just suppose that some of us have become a bit too comfortable down here. Does that make sense?"

Mr Berkley nodded, but Jack thought the man didn't make sense at all.

"Well, I hope you have a nice day today." Chuck said, leaving the table abruptly.

As the man walked away, Mr Berkley smiled at the two boys.

Jack ate quickly; he was eager to look through the glass panels in the floor, for he had overheard someone speaking about an angler fish which had drifted right beneath the thick perimeter.

As Jack reclined on a glass floor, a girl's voice jingled from beside him: "Morning Jack. Have *you* seen that creature Jet was talkin' about?"

"Good morning! No, I was just looking for it now." Jack explained, looking to Lucy. She wore a bright-green blouse and sweat pants. Her hair was let down and a slightly tangled. "How was your night?"

"Oh, it was just fine," she replied, "the room was very cozy. I thought it was like the submarines, the way it was furnished."

"So did I." Jack said. "Did your room have a fish tank like ours?"

"It did. One of the fish was dead, though. It was a sad sight." she stated, kneeling on the floor beside the Wesley boy.

"That's a shame," Jack said, "the people here seem awfully busy, don't they?"

Lucy nodded. "They sure do," she replied, "but they don't seem to mind it."

"They must make a lotta money." Jack stated, transfixing his gaze on a far-off S.A.P. crawling about the chasm below. "Something is worrying me about my father, Lucy." he blurted.

She shuffled her knees, coming closer. "What is it?" she whispered.

"I have this feeling that he *hasn't* been building robots all this time," he explained, "when he started working more often, I figured that he was just dealing with losing mother. But, I began to realize that there was something here that he cared about more than Genoa–more than me." Jack's head hung as he spoke.

Lucy then asked, "What do you know about your dad's work?"

He explained more quietly, "He is a manager, so I would assume he is in charge of Incandium's business. But, there was information onboard my submarine about some 'Wesley and Verne' project, and it just didn't seem to line up. I *tried* to learn more about the project, but the Auto Pilot said that I needed a pass-phrase."

"Jack," Lucy said, hitting the glass with her fist, "hear me out, you *have to* get to the bottom of this. This is your chance to confront your father; you ought to ask him how important his work is to him, and whether it's worth neglecting the incredible boy that is his son."

Jack was about to thank the girl when a strange bulb of blindingly white light passed beneath the floor. A monster followed. "It's so ugly!" Lucy cried.

Mr Berkley stood above the two with his arms crossed. "That's why it hides in the dark." he said.

Chapter Nine
The Secret

Ned spoke through his megaphone and sent the islanders back to the lodgings.

As he entered into the lobby, Jack spotted his father dashing through the corridor. The boy spied around a pillar to see the white-coated man slip through one of the hallway doors. Jack wandered towards this particular door before being quickly halted. "You! Boy, come this way." the orange-coated man demanded, clearly irate about the investigation attempt.

A basket of assorted fruits and chocolates sat on the black sheets of the lodging's bed when Jack came into the room. A complimentary tag was observed on the wooden handle: "Welcome back, valued employee." Sam laughed when his brother showed him the message.

The brothers played with their yo-yos, competed at chess, and surveyed the room.

The hours passed by slowly until an unidentified employee unlocked the lodging's door. Genoa's people flooded through the Sub Port halls and the cafeteria was suddenly full again. Chuck was sitting with company, so Jack, Sam, and the lighthouse man found their own table.

"Say, this pie is remarkable." Mr Berkley asserted, after having plunged into dessert.

Lucy was busy, but some colorful jellyfish kept Jack company after lunch was finished. The boy watched from a glass flooring as the orange-coated man went into the kitchen. "Now's my chance." he thought. After quietly leaving the cafeteria, he passed by the lobby. No soul lingered, but Jack knew he had little time to spare. He began running past the doors. Door after door after door he passed. Finally, he came to the passage he believed he had seen his father enter through. It was slightly opened. He reached out towards the handle, but the door suddenly swung open, knocking Jack backwards.

"Oh! I'm sorry." came a surprised voice. Dr Verne stood aghast. "Aren't you one of Dr Wesley's children?" he slowly asked, tilting his head and pointing a finger at Jack.

The boy nodded and answered, "Yes sir, I am."

"Can I help you find something?" the doctor briskly inquired, slamming the door and then locking it with a gold key.

"No sir," Jack answered, "I was simply looking around."

The president scratched his nose and adjusted his jacket. It seemed to Jack that he could have been a sharp and sensible man, but something had changed him over these years. "You know kid–you are *not* supposed to leave the cafeteria."

"I am sorry, sir," Jack said, "I'll go back."

"Enjoy your lunch." Dr Verne sneered, shoeing Jack away with a hand gesture.

The Wesley boy's heart raced when he was near the man, but he now knew that he must see what was on the other side of the door; something in room one fifty-one concerned both his father *and* Dr Verne.

Jack came back to find an employee orating to the people about a complimentary medical office near the lobby. The black and teal-green megaphone was then used to announce the ending of lunch.

For the second time that day, Sam failed to defend himself against his brother's attacks; Jack's knights were much more useful than he had assumed.

•

John stood beside a slanted panel. He was turning off the cafeteria's electrical power, as he did every day around this time. It was at this series of colorful buttons and plastic switches that he and his colleague could control the Sub Port like puppeteers pulling on the stings of a puppet. John lifted a glass hood to find a black button labeled, "Self Destruct." He sighed and covered the button back up. "One o'clock, one o'clock." he muttered to himself, "where's Dr Verne?" He looked to the short hole in the wall of the grotto where he and his colleague had secretly transported supplies from the boathouse. Although the president was mad, John could not deny his brilliant shrewdness.

A triangle of yellow light expanded and then retracted upon the floor of dark-grey and brown. "You're free." Dr Verne announced, stepping off the ladder. Coming closer, he said, "I'm not sure why, but your son was snooping around the hallway." "John," he said, in a serious tone, "he almost went into room one fifty-one."

"Was it Jack or Sam?" John inquired, turning from the Sub Port's controls.

"The dark-haired one." the president described, "he was on his own."

"I'll talk to him about it later."

"You best make sure he stays put." Dr Verne insisted. "So, what's the plan for tonight?"

John stretched his back and replied, "We are throwing a Christmas party." He smiled and explained, "There will be turkey with stuffing, gelatin, hot chocolate, you know, those kinds of things."

"Marvelous." Dr Verne said, sarcastically. "Any more buzzing noises?"

"Didn't notice any."

Incandium Science Labs' founder walked across the room like a prisoner returning to his cell after recess. "During your break, you ought to check in with Ned," he said, "I heard him speaking with a guard about us again. We don't want him getting any ideas."

•

A white envelope slipped beneath the white door

of the lodge. Sam picked it up and read it. "There will be a Christmas party tonight." he stated.

Mr Berkley grinned and said, "How pleasant. I just assumed that they didn't celebrate the holiday season down here."

Sam said, "It starts at seven."

Jack was already to the door. "It's unlocked." he remarked, twisting the knob. Slipping on his dark-blue jacket, he asked, "Can I meet you two down there?" They nodded at each other and then at Jack. He swung open the door and jogged to the elevator.

He stood alone in the red and gold room. The elevator opened to the sound of Christmas tunes. Jogging out of the lobby, Jack spied down the corridor to find yellow tape spanning the gap and two bulky guard men pacing in the distance. "Jiminy!" he muttered. "Dr Verne is sure serious about keeping people out of that room." he thought.

Jack came to the cafeteria. Sitting at a table with a red and green tablecloth, he observed a poster hanging on the dome: "PROGRESS."

Three men and two women walked around the room. They were holding various decorations and wore frowns. Jack frowned too, watching them with half-closed eyes.

"My name is Georgie, I will be serving you tonight. Will there be more joining you?" said a brunette wearing a red apron.

"Yes, two others." Jack said.

"Would you like a refreshment?" the waitress asked.

"Do you have a cherry soda?"

"Of course we do, sir." she answered.

"I'll take one, please."

"I'll be right back with it."

Sam and Mr Berkley joined Jack at the circular table. A glass of fizzy, pink liquid was placed beside a bouquet of roses. "May I have one of those?" Sam asked the lady in the red apron, pointing to Jack's drink. Mr Berkley then asked for fruit punch.

Soon, many of Genoa's islanders sat at the tables, waiting for the main course.

Ned came up to the kitchen and, holding up his megaphone, spoke to the people. "Good evening," he cheered, "tonight, Incandium wants to treat its special guests with a Christmas dinner. We do hope you enjoy."

The three friends ate steaming turkey with cranberry sauce, fluffy bread, and blue gelatin desert.

John surprised them by visiting their table. "Good evening!" he greeted.

Jack raised his fork and knife. "Father!" he exclaimed.

The grey-haired engineer cracked a smile; the faces of these three made him feel admittedly content. "How is dinner?" he asked. They all agreed that it was exceptional. "For once, the meal was prepared by humans!" he explained, laughing.

Sam asked, "Are you eating with us?"

His father tilted his head and then responded, "No, I'm planning on eating later on."

"May I ask why," Mr Berkley inquired, "do you

have work to do?"

"Yes, I do." he answered, forcing a laugh. He awkwardly rubbed the back of his neck. "Boy, do I wish you could've come another time. You don't know how badly I want to be with you three."

"Is that so?" Jack asked. "What kind of work are you doing at *this* hour?"

"I better not say exactly." the father explained. He stared into a red checker on the Christmassy tablecloth and whispered, "What we are working on is–extraordinary."

Jack quietly asked, "Is it in room one fifty-one?"

John looked around, hoping that their conversation had been a private one. (He regretted saying as much as he had.) "I need to make sure no one goes in that room," John declared, clenching his jaw, "especially you, Jack! It's too dangerous."

"'Dangerous'?" Jack retorted mockingly.

Mr Berkley put down his silverware and looked to the engineer. "We sure wish you could eat with us, John, but I suppose we will have to do without you." Looking at the Wesley boys, he said, "We understand your work is important."

John thanked them.

Haunting memories of boat trips and dinners without his father consumed Jack's mind. He stood up, glaring at his father across the table. "I hope that this 'extraordinary' creation is worth your relationship with your children! And, if what you're working on is so incredible, why do you keep it a secret?" Tears streaked his cheeks and fell off his chin. "There is so much I've wanted to tell you."

John's conscience burned within, yet he refused to speak. The aged man was unable to bear what he was feeling. He needed to return to something familiar. As an audience watched from nearby tables, John buttoned his jacket and left for the grotto. He was tired, and thirsty.

Jack spent much of the evening alone in the lodging. He had left the party soon after his father had visited. Mr Berkley came in to comfort him. "We can trust God's timing," his blue-vested godfather explained, "things will work out. Remember, we have to face the good *and* the bad."

"We're not facing anything by being so weak and passive," Jack asserted, "we need to do something!"

"Right now, there's nothing we can do, my lad." Mr Berkley acknowledged.

☾

Like clockwork, the doors unlocked and the people left. Soon came aromas of bleach and berries and coffee.

Breakfast found Jack and Lucy in the cafeteria. Despite the Sub Port's wonder and curiosity, Jack assumed that his experiences at Incandium's headquarters would pollute his memories of his undersea adventure. "I did it. I confronted my father," he told Lucy after saying hello, "but, there is no hope for us."

The girl seemingly understood Jack's situation.

She took time to answer, fiddling with her ponytail for several moments. "I don't tell many friends about it," she said, "but my father used to mistreat me badly. He was a horrendous drunk, and, some nights, he would come home from fishing with this strange look in his eyes; he brought home the troubles and worries from his work at sea and would yell at me for things I didn't do.

"But, I learned to trust that he didn't *really* mean what he said. If you'd ask me, I'd say that your father is making some serious decisions right now and you will have to have faith that he is going to make the right ones."

Jack had a sharp pain in his throat; he wanted to believe her. Pointing towards the dismal armed guards in the distant hallway, he declared, "I'm not sure if it's worth the risk. I know what I have to do, but I don't know if I can do it."

Lucy looked at Jack in his tear-filled eyes. "You *can* do it."

☾

The Sub Port's cellar, a room with a low ceiling and full of wine bottles, was where John was asked to meet Dr Verne. John thought the reef walls were intimidating, and Timothy Hayes probably did too.

"Tim, what happened?" asked John. He was only aquatinted with Mr Hays; he knew him to visit Genoa during his winter sailing expeditions.

"That man—the one in the orange coat," Timothy

explained, "he whipped me straight."

Dr Verne joined the two in the alcohol reserve. "Ah, Tim." he muttered. He then kicked the frightened sailor's stool so that they faced each other. "Why the trouble?" he inquired, trying to appear calm. Timothy fell back into his seat as Dr Verne picked something up from the ground. Timothy gazed at the thing; it was a long metal club with an inscription of a snake at the tip. The scientist continued: "Do you want to go back up there? You really want to trade perfection for–for filth? I don't see how you could not be satisfied."

The man wore a confused face; he looked to John and then to Dr Verne. "Sir, Doctor, I just want to know when I can see my family again. Is that too much to ask?"

Dr Verne walked up to a wall, spun on his heels, and then came back to Timothy, hammering the club against the metal table he sat at. "Yes, it *is* too much to ask. And, if this happens again, it's going to be a lot worse. John, take care of the rest." The megalomaniac stormed out of the room, taking a bottle of red wine with him.

John deeply wished that he could simply let his island-dwelling friends leave. But, he had already made the choice: he could not let anyone go until the time vessel had taken all of the power that it needed to work–and there wasn't enough left for everyone else.

Timothy leaned across the table, clanking the cuffs that were locked to his chair. "John," he whispered, "what has gotten into you? What has become of the man I used to know? Don't you know what it's like to want to see your children again? Don't you know what it can be like to—"

"Quiet!" John yelled. His gaze shifted to the bewildered prisoner. "I'm sorry, I just need to know that you won't try anything stupid again. I promise that you will see your family soon. We are just dealing with—urgent matters."

Despite Tim appearing unsatisfied with his answers, John sent the sailor on his way after instructing an employee to unlock the cuffs. The engineer then returned to the grotto.

Dr Verne was elsewhere—possibly in his spacious lounge recounting money or sending telegrams to various military clients. John bent over and picked up the leather suitcase Mr Berkley had given him. He unbuckled the latches and opened the bag on an uneven table. A shiny object of Newtonian crafts-manship resided with notebooks and picture frames. "The telescope." he muttered. A tear fell down his face and onto the treasured object. A note lay on the glass creation.

"*My friend John,*

"*I want to remind you of a time when work wasn't quite so important—a time when an island was all you needed. We would swim in the rivers and explore the coast. Do you remember?*

"*Some of us are on a ship, looking for our way through life. Others are on the other side, and we shine our lights to lead the way. John, I can only imagine how hard things are for you. But we both know that you have lost your way. I hope you can come back to the lighthouse and take your children on those trails that we would roam as young men. You know Marie would have wanted that."*

"Cordially, Mr Berkley."

•

"I have this feeling," Mr Thompson told Mr Berkley at lunch, "that the storm has passed. How quickly did you say that hurricane was moving? Yes, it should have passed by now. Don't you think we should ask someone if they have the report?"

Mr Berkley wiped his mouth with his napkin and nodded. "I would say that's a good idea."

Mr Thompson then said, "Some men on my floor seemed quite upset last night. They are growing tired of being locked in their rooms. It's been hard on my family, too. The place is too small for us."

Jack sat at the table; he could relate.

"I am sure that they will let us go soon. They seem well-informed, so they should know when the storm has passed." Mr Berkley said, with some assurance in his manner.

"I will check in with you later. *Do* try to get a report soon, though." the fellow islander requested, leaving the table.

"Bye, pal."

That afternoon, Mr Berkley was curtly denied his request of the weather report. The Wesley brothers noticed that this frustrated the lighthouse man.

"There are armed guards in those halls, Mr Berkley," a woman from Genoa explained to the lighthouse man in the lobby, "this is a laboratory, not the White House!"

"I'm sorry, Miss Louis," the lighthouse man condoled, "I am not entirely sure why they are taking such measures. I trust you'll be safe."

"It is my children I am worried about. Who knows what could happen if they ran off into some room?" she said, pointing towards the hallway.

Mr Berkley scratched his head. "Maybe I can put in a word for you." He smiled and the woman walked away.

Around three o'clock in the afternoon, Jack and Sam were disturbed by loud noises coming from beyond the lodgings: yelling and clanking.

"Tim Hayes got in a fight with some employees," Mr Berkley explained to the brothers that evening, "he regrets it now, I'm sure. But, I suppose we can't blame him for wanting to get back to his family."

"I suppose not." said Sam.

Seafood had been prepared for dinner. Most of the fishermen were impressed by the meal although none would dare say that the robot chefs did any better with the halibut than they could.

An armed man approached Mr Berkley and the Wesleys after dinner. "Jack, right?" he asked, alarming the boy. "Please come with me." he said.

Jack silently looked to his two friends before following the guard. The man wore black slacks, white shoulder-plates, and a white helmet. He had a gun on his hip, and several other devices lined his pant legs. He took Jack to the side of the cafeteria opposite the kitchen. "My name is Donny." he said. He was obviously nervous; his fingers twitched and his lips quivered. But, he had a charming persona that Jack found to be disarming. "You've been sneaking around room one fifty-one, right?"

Jack shamefully nodded.

"You are trying to figure out what your old man's up to, eh?"

"Well, yes, I am actually."

"Look at this, sport." he said, quickly unfolding a piece of blue paper that had rested in a pant pocket. It became apparent that this man was on Jack's side.

"A blueprint?"

"Not just any blueprint," the guard said, excitedly, "this looks like a time machine!"

"Pardon?" inquired the Wesley boy.

"A while ago, I overheard your dad talking to Dr Verne about some kind of project. Look here. They call it the 'time vessel.' I did some investigation and it seems as though they've been working on it for a long time."

"The 'time vessel.'" Jack repeated. He had only read of such a thing in fictional stories.

Donny whispered now: "I have reason to dislike the president, you see. Trust me when I say he is a villain; he knows how to get by with all kinds of evil. But, we can finally bust him this time: Verne is breaking the rules by working on an *unauthorized* project. And somehow, I think you and I are the only ones who know that *something* is going on here. Jack, do you want to help me?"

The brown-haired boy looked up to Donny. An unending mystery could finally be solved. With a newfound courage, Jack answered, "Yes," and shook the guard's hand.

"I have a shift tomorrow," he explained, "and we are going to get into that room! You can't tell anyone that you're in on this, understand?"

Jack nodded.

"I'm just telling you not to spy on the hallway doors anymore, right?" he asked, winking.

Jack nodded once more and then rushed off. His head spun. Lucy would be thrilled.

"What was that all about?" Mr Berkley asked as Jack sat back down at the table.

"He was just scolding me about spying around in the hallway." Jack replied.

"Those guards *are* armed, you know."

•

"You're free." Dr Verne announced, stepping off the ladder and then walking across the grotto floor.

The time vessel hummed uncontrollably, and the engineer was found leaning over an open suitcase.

"You're free, John, didn't you hear me?" the president asked with a chuckle.

Looking at Dr Verne, John saw a monster. Only now, with a changed mind, could he see the man for who he really was.

"You're right, I am free." he remarked, carefully setting down the telescope he held. He ran at Dr Verne and they tumbled onto the hard floor.

"Ah! John, what are you doing?" Dr Verne gasped as John began to choke him.

The strangling man desperately reached his arm out towards his legs and revealed a glimmering knife. John changed his grip, but the blade plunged deep into his side. He screamed in pain. Dr Verne now stood above him. He began pulling his colleague across the floor.

Something crashed in the distance, distracting the fighters. While Dr Verne was looking away, John rose to his feet and wandered towards the panel of colorful buttons and plastic switches. He was about to shut off the time vessel's power when Dr Verne jumped on top of him. "No! No!" he shouted.

Dr Verne angrily shoved John into a tiny, dark closet at the grotto's perimeter. The president was trembling and whining. Into the wooden enclosure, Dr Verne cried: "I can't believe this. And after all these years! Tomorrow, we were going to explore history together, John, how could you?"

Dr Wesley was bleeding all over the floor. He fell asleep.

Chapter Ten
An Escape

It was ten in the morning and the door was still locked. Breakfast was delivered by two guards who wore white hats. Our hopeful friend waited anxiously for Donny. Today, the guests were told, there would be a lockdown at the Sub Port; no one would be allowed to leave his room. Only trouble could follow and everyone knew it.

"Boy was breakfast better in the cafe." Sam complained as he spooned cold oatmeal from a plastic bowl.

Jack was watching the red fish as they swam through apertures in the tank's reef structures. His mind had been reeling since the unveiling of the perplexing blueprints. If Donny was honest and his father had helped Dr Verne build a time machine, then Jack could now begin to understand the obsession. "What if," thought Jack, "father has built this machine only to be with mother again?" The Wesley boy was motionless. A swirling spiral of red and blue tempted him to dream not of Genoa, nor of the great blue whale, but of his mother. Her tenderness and her love were captivating. "Father has not been so selfish all along," he realized in an epiphany, "oh, poor father!" Yet, how badly the engineer wished to be with his old friend Jack could never fathom.

Sam and Mr Berkley were feverishly playing chess when the door finally cracked open. "Hello?" asked a friendly voice.

Jack left the fish tank and came to the door.

"Hello, it's Donny," the man said, sticking his head through the doorway, "we must leave now!"

Sam and Mr Berkley joined Jack at the door. "What is this about?" demanded the Wesleys' guardian.

"He's taking me to father." Jack explained.

"Listen, you two need to prepare to evacuate," Donny commanded with a shaking voice, "it turns out that the storm has passed, and Dr Verne has been harnessing the Sub Port's power for a secret project with no real plan to release Genoa's people! Once we disable his machine, your friends will be able to leave. If you will allow it, sir, I will take the lad with me."

Mr Berkley rubbed his forehead. "I don't believe this," he remarked, "will he be safe?"

"I can't promise that, sir, but he *will* be useful." Looking at Jack, Donny stated, "He will help rescue the people of your island."

Jack waited for an answer from the thoughtful Mr Berkley.

"Godspeed, then." said the lighthouse.

Sam said goodbye as Jack hurried out the door. "I wasn't sure if you'd still be coming!" Jack exclaimed as the two rushed into an elevator and began descending to the first floor. They snuck past an employee in the lobby and then came to room one fifty-one.

Donny looked to his left and then to his right and then revealed a gold key. "You have no idea how hard it was for me to get this." Incandium's double-crossing employee remarked.

"It's just an empty room!" Jack declared, stepping inside a white construction of blank walls and scattered equipment.

"That's what they want you to think." Donny said, smiling. He walked up to a small cabinet and reached inside. Pulling some sort of chord, he caused a few tiles in the floor to open like a triangular cardboard box.

"Once we take care of Dr Verne, your father can help us leave." Stopping beside the opening in the floor, Donny explained, "Your father looked like he was in bad shape last I saw him. I just don't want you to be disappointed, sport."

Jack wasn't sure exactly what Donny meant, but, before he could say knife, he was given a handgun and shoved inside. The guard asked the islander whether he knew how to shoot such a weapon. He cocked the handgun and nodded.

A crackling radio accompanying an accented voice approached the door. "Who are they?" Jack whispered.

"The Red Ones," replied Donny, sternly, "hurry, climb down as fast as you can."

The doorknob was turning.

"What about you?"

"Farewell, Jack." wished Donny.

Another pull of the chord sent the tiles back over the Wesley boy. Shouting ensued.

Jack's heart thumped within his chest. The investigation was futile. Courage was dangerous.

He climbed down the aperture hastily and his steps echoed. The darkness became a yellowish shade of grey as Jack entered into a strange room. A grotto. The place was somewhat reminiscent of the submarine boathouse on Genoa. Lingering in the surrounding shadows were torn canvas illustrations, contorted prototypes, glass bottles, and scraps of rubbish. In the center, Jack viewed a large box. It was hard for him to take his eyes off of the outlandish, blue thing. "The time vessel." he thought. As he walked towards the machine, he perceived an intense blast of electric power reverberating through the air. The place appeared to be void of people. As he walked about the floor, he sighted empty liquor bottles and food scraps lying about.

A shadow moved in the distance. Jack halted. Holding his breath, he found the handgun on his belt. Dr Verne stepped out from behind the time vessel and shouted, "You!"

The Wesley boy froze, as though he had just come back out of the cold water at Genoa's port.

"Jack?" asked Incandium's president. "That *is* your name, isn't it?"

Jack asked in a quiet voice, "Where is my father?"

"He is taking a break right now." Dr Verne fabricated.

"Did you know about the storm all along?" the Wesley boy questioned.

"The storm?"

Jack saw dark-red liquid dripping from a wooden enclosure nearby. He also noticed that he wasn't the only one in the standoff with a gun.

"Just—walk toward me." Dr Verne said.

"Why is there blood on your hands?" Jack whispered, anger boiling.

Dr Verne put his hands behind his back and looked to the closet.

"What did you do to my father?" Jack yelled furiously.

Dr Verne's left hand went for his belt, but Jack was ready first. Two shrill gunshots blasted through the rocky chasm and Dr Verne fell to the rocky floor. Having shot first, Jack was spared by a few feet.

The boy was utterly dazed. He slowly placed his gun on his belt and walked towards the closet. He stopped to glance at Dr Verne. He had been shot in the stomach and was moaning loudly as he lay there. Jack picked up the man's silver pistol and set it on a table.

There was a lock on the closet door when Jack examined it. "Father." he said. "Father!" Picking up a heavy piece of sharp metal, he began pounding the lock. The door eventually came open. Jack found a body lying in a puddle of blood. Bending over with tears in his eyes, he was relieved to see that his father was breathing. The boy hurriedly took the tape off the engineer's mouth.

"Jack." he gasped.

"Are you able to walk?" the Wesley boy asked, trembling as he untied the ropes which were tightly knotted around his wrists and ankles.

John stumbled several times as he crossed the floor. Turning to his son, he said, "You are *so* brave." He embraced the teenager tightly. "I've let you down," he cried, "you can never forgive me!"

Jack then declared, "Yes, I can! Oh, it must have been so hard for you." Wrapping his arms around his father's blood-stained coat, he asked, "You built this so that you could be with mother again, didn't you?"

The grey-haired man nodded. He was crying.

"We need to turn it off," Jack stated, "it's the only way we can get the people back to the surface."

Jack and his injured father came to the grotto's control panel. "No," John shouted when his son reached for the termination button, "let me do it." The man reached for the button and then took his hand back.

"Are you okay, father?" Jack asked.

He was thinking about Marie. Her black locks. Her crystal eyes. He then turned to see the incredible creation, finally ready. Marie waited just beyond the metal walls of the time machine. "Let's get out of here!" he yelled, smiling wide.

The machine's lights flickered and then turned off. As whirling noises descended into a fading hum, the time vessel died. The grotto was considerably quiet now. A gentle sound of dripping water echoed through the chandelier-lit cavern.

Dr Verne lay on the ground, gasping.

"Tie him up to a chair—with these." John commanded Jack, holding out some rope.

Incandium's president murmured as Jack lifted him by his armpits and then tied him to the chair. Mr Berkley had taught him many knots, but his memory was failing him.

"We need to get moving!" John exclaimed.

Jack finished what he thought was a bowline knot. Incandium's president remained quiet; his world must have been crashing all around him. His head hung low. The chair was turned toward his treasured invention, and he inadvertently bowed to the one thing that had consumed him.

After collecting some things, John asked Jack to carry the leather suitcase. The engineer climbed the ladder rather slowly, and his son stopped several times to help him.

Four bodies lay on the floor in room one fifty-one. Donny had stopped the Red Ones from getting to Jack, but the heroic endeavor cost him his life.

"Donny!" Jack cried. "He's dead."

John stayed near his son. "He did his job." he comforted.

"He saved me," Jack whispered, glancing at the three deceased strangers who wore bright-red suits, "and he took them all down himself." Jack turned to his father. "What can I do for you?" he asked.

"Help me push that shelf over the trapdoor. We

need to make sure Verne stays put."

After obstructing the passageway, John told his son, "Get Sam and Mr Berkley. I will sound the alarm."

"Yes sir," Jack replied, "will you be alright? You look badly hurt."

"I'll be fine for now," he said, "let's meet in the pier at noon." "I love you, son. I love you so much."

"I love you too, father." said Jack before leaving for his room. As he rode in the elevator, he heard his father speaking over the telecom: "This is a message from Dr John Wesley. We are now evacuating the people of Genoa. The storm has passed and the people can leave. Housing squad, unlock all lodging doors and escort our guests to the boathouse. Workers and all other employees, cancel your projects and prepare all our submarines for immediate departure."

As Jack traversed towards his lodging, he realized that power was restored to the facility; the air became colder and the lights, brighter.

Jack was kindly greeted by his friends. "We heard the message. It seems that you have helped to bring your father to his senses," said Mr Berkley, smiling warmly, "we've packed your bag for you." "How is he, anyway?"

"I think he's been hurt. But he will be okay." Jack stated.

"Praise God." Mr Berkley declared. "And good riddance." he remarked, closing the door to their prison of a room.

In the lobby, Jack overheard a woman relating to a man in a jumpsuit: "Did you hear? Dr Verne is quite the shuck after all! We should've known that he's been up to something–he hasn't been producing as many blueprints as he used to." "They say Dr Wesley might have been in on it too. It must have been quite a project; unauthorized undertakings are quite the offense in *this* business."

Streaming colors of obedient employees flashed through the Sub Port maze; they carried boxes of food and supplies.

"So, you followed Donny into room one five one– and then what happened?" Ned asked Jack. The two were inside the Sub Port's alerting room found above the lobby. (The Wesley boy had been called to answer questions about the day's dangerous developments.)

"He gave me a gun and sent me down through the trapdoor," Jack recalled, "once I was in the hidden room, I looked around. Then, Dr Verne came out. He told me to come to him, but I saw him reaching for the gun on his belt. I took my gun and shot him as fast as I could."

"That's it?" Ned asked, tapping his pen on a stack of paper. The mountain on his arm had a snowy cap.

"That's it."

Jack was sent out of the room. His father replaced him and had a long discussion about something seemingly weighty. As John left the room, Ned told him, "You don't have to thank me. You know Who *really* forgave you."

Jack's father explained to him that he was being pardoned for his affiliation with the creation of a secret machine. Dr Verne would be reported dead after suffering a heart attack.

Sam stopped Jack in the hallway. "Wait up, Jack, so you shot him with a handgun?" the curious boy whispered, wearing an utterly bewildered face.

"Yes," Jack replied as an employee walked past them, "but, we can talk about it later."

John was wrapping a towel around his wound when he sighted Mr Berkley enter into the boathouse through the wooden doors. He tied a knot with the towel and then hurried to his friend. "You saved me," he cried, "you brought me out that despicable cave and I am forever thankful."

Mr Berkley just smiled.

"I know you won't take my money," John said, "but, I need to know what I can do in return."

The lighthouse man gestured down the corridor, towards John's children. "Your boys–they need you more than ever," he said, "and they've had enough of me. Besides, I've been saving for a vacation in the Caribbean."

John nodded and then hugged Mr Berkley, thanking him once more.

Ned, John, Mr Thompson, and Mr Berkley led the evacuation. Before long, several submarines were fully charged and their tanks were full of fuel. The people of Genoa were setting a course for the coast of north California.

The lighthouse man sat on a pile of baggage,

wiping his forehead with a handkerchief. "Boys, we've really done it," he cheered, "we saved our people and are now we are headed to our new home!"

"We've done it all right!" Jack exclaimed. He looked at one of his hands; he was still shaking.

"I couldn't have imagined that all this would happen," Mr Berkley explained sincerely, "but we served our people loyally, and, you two will never forget this incredible story!"

"What's that alarm for?" Sam inquired, popping his head out of a nearby mountain of luggage. A low-pitched siren blasted overhead.

John ran towards the wooden doors. "No, no, no!" he shrieked.

As murmurs spread throughout the boathouse, various lights shut off and the fuel-dispensers ran dry. "Dr Verne is on the move." John whispered to himself. Through intercoms, his voice came urgently: "The Sub Port has just become a time bomb! I need every man, woman, and child in the boathouse right now! The self-destruction bomb has been triggered and it will initiate in thirty minutes or less."

Seven of the ten submarines were arranged for departure. There were no longer options or accom-modations; *everyone* had to leave immediately.

Sam found Jack and, together, they scurried about, helping however they could. Babies cried, men shouted, women screamed. The scene was, in Jack's opinion, more disturbing than that of Genoa's evacuation.

"What in heavens do you need that for?" a sailor

inquired of a wiry man about an oddly-shaped crate full of seeds. "I think you ought to do a little to help before you start loading on your little seeds."

"These aren't just seeds–they are scientific discoveries, and they need to stay safe!" came the defensive reply.

Amidst the chaos, the question the workers asked was clear: What would life be like outside of the incredible Sub Port? Certain employees hurried through the laboratory, lingering for several minutes; they sought to bring with them some of the revolutionary inventions they had created under the supervision of a genius. A few individuals needed to clarify with John that the bomb was inviolable once triggered. The employees were entirely pitiful; some cried and others conversed with each other about their terrible dilemma.

Mr Berkley halted his helping to ask for John the whereabouts of Dr Verne.

"He is in the grotto," John said, "and he has nowhere to go."

Mr Berkley looked at John with a pacific expression and said, "Very well, then."

Whether he was actually still alive John did not know. In observation of a new power-outage, it seemed to him that the president had turned the time machine back on.

Upon John's request, Genoa's people left first. One by one, the submarines departed, their voyagers hastily thanking the lighthouse man for his leadership and Incandium's residents for their hospitality.

Mr Thompson had to intervene when a middle-aged man attempted to strike a sailor upon a joke being made about the sad state of the Sub Port's workers. The employee's wrists were tied together before he was placed in a submarine reserved for Incandium personnel.

At noon, two submarines were left in the boathouse. The final voyagers were the executive employees at the Sub Port and the few that we've become so acquainted with: Jack, Sam, and Mr Berkley. In the islanders' submarine also came Pete the grocer and the Thompson family. John respected his people and was adamant on being the last one to leave, regardless of who joined him.

As the sixth submarine departed, Mr Berkley stood with John on the marble floor. "I'll help get your boys' baggage onboard," Mr Berkley said, "you can get the sub started up."

The potted cacti stood with their arms pointed towards the sky and the fresh air that the islanders missed. Jack rolled his suitcase along the floor as Mr Berkley helped carry Sam's second duffle. The sirens' wailing was a de ja vu for the islanders who had just evacuated a mere week before.

"Sam," said Jack, as they jogged across the dock, "thank you for joining me on this adventure."

"Any time, pal," the boy-turned-adult coolly replied, "any time."

Mr Berkley accidentally dropped his handkerchief on the marble floor. He stopped to pick it up.

Meanwhile, John was initiating the Auto Pilot. He pulled the towel up his side to view the gash in his flesh; he flinched from a terrible pain. "Five minutes, five minutes." he said. "Where are the boys?"

An alarming blast was then heard coming from the short hole in the far wall. A four-wheeled cargo-cart fell over, spilling aluminum sheets and uncovering a bloody Dr Verne who crawled out of the mysterious tunnel.

Mr Berkley tucked his handkerchief into one of his vest pockets. "Boys," he said calmly, "get inside that sub right now."

Coming off the ground, Dr Verne screamed, "David Berkley! You took everything from me!"

The brothers threw their bags into the hatch opening and climbed up the side of the sail as quickly as they could. Expecting Mr Berkley to be following closely behind, Jack turned from the top of the sail to see that the lighthouse man had stayed where he was on the marble dock. "Mr Berkley!" he cried. Sam pulled on Jack's shirt and ordered him to get inside. But, Jack would not take his eyes off of his godfather.

Mr Berkley turned from Dr Verne to see his younger friend from home. "Show your father the life he deserves." were his last words.

Incandium's president lifted his handgun.

"No!" screamed Jack.

Two gunshots fired and the lighthouse man was hit twice. Mr Berkley fell onto the marble floor. Dr Verne's handgun was then raised toward the brothers.

"Jack!" screamed Sam, before the president's fire smashed the hatch-door.

Jack helped his brother close the hatch and then fell onto the metal floor in dismay. Sam sprinted to the control room.

"Where is Mr Berkley?" John asked, as his son rancorously rushed into the control room. Sam just cried. "Where is he?" repeated the father, ignorantly.

Jack, fearing that Dr Verne would attempt to continue his rampage, stood up and peered out through the sail porthole. He watched as the megalomaniac scientist stood over Mr Berkley and then turned away. He limped through the wooden doors and back into his marvelous kingdom. He was never seen again.

Mr Berkley lay on the marble dock, peacefully sleeping. Jack didn't want to look at him, but he could not take his gaze off the hero. He stared until the submarine sank to safety beneath the Sub Port's deathly claws. The facility's lights soon shut off, leaving the metallic vessel in a dark abyss.

Jack and Sam met in the living quarter, silently watching a clock tick or a pencil roll across a table. Later, Jack left to cry in the bathroom; he was terribly grieved. Shortly after the submarine exited the underwater tunnel of scientific discovery and forgotten achievement, the Sub Port exploded. The room which had danced in beautiful colors now danced in colors of hope and freedom.

A new home awaited.

Chapter Eleven
Mountains and Prairies

John was suffering from a new mental battle as the submarine drifted eastward. "Why did David have to die?" he asked himself. "And why didn't I think of the passageway into the boathouse?" His sons comforted him, though, and explained that Mr Berkley would have never wanted him to be so hard on himself; they told him the man's final words and how he was so gallant when he faced Dr Verne. The engineer understood that the lighthouse man's death would forevermore be a burden to carry.

Like his many coworkers, John faced the question about life outside of the undersea laboratory. It was a life he never dared return to after Marie's passing. But, there was nowhere left to go anymore, and he was beginning to accept that.

For many hours after leaving the Sub Port, the Wesley children found themselves in utter dismay. The quiet reverberations of the vibraphone tunes were almost comforting; the notes rose slowly, then came back down suddenly, like the bright and bubbling colors of strange emotion that boiled up within the boys.

Jack remembered the sunny, windy afternoons he would spend teasing Mr Berkley.

"Almost there!" he and Sam would each yell from the grey boulders on the hillside.

"You know I can't get up there!" he would say, before fixing his vest or pushing his hair to the side.

Mrs Thompson, who proved to be a handy seamstress, was quick to sterilize and stitch John's wound the day they left the Sub Port. John thanked her and then fetched medicine from a bathroom closet. The father then fell asleep in one of the control room's swivel chairs.

John stayed in the control room for most of the voyage. It was a good place for him to contemplate, to reason with himself.

The Wesley brothers didn't speak much to their fellow voyagers, yet they were polite and played games with the Thompsons.

Jack noticed after several observations that Mr Thompson was unhappy with the sacrifice Mr Berkley made. For one reason or another, the once-mailman had made up his mind that John wasn't deserving of such redemption. Jack could relate to his position, as they had both known the lighthouse man so well. In good time, Jack decided, things would make more sense.

~

It was a truly amusing scene as loads of refugees and private corporation scientists arrived in California in submersibles of unforeseen technological advancements. They came to Port Verne, a harbor that had been reserved for Sub Port workers. The islanders were overjoyed to be above the ocean's surface. However, the members of Incandium were like fish out of water.

Soon, it would be Christmas Day, and many of the families were desperate to find a place to settle in. The wind was spicy and the sun, hidden by dense clouds.

"Where will we go now?" asked a trader in a thick, Spanish accent.

After speaking to many of the islanders, John found a solution: Felix Meriwether (a mailman who had lived on Genoa) had a friend who owned a hotel in the area. Mr Meriwether would call to ask the man if there was space available for, "ninety-one guests, give or take."

It was then evening, and Felix was still gone at the phone station with his bag of nickels. Families huddled under blankets as John paced the creaky docks. From the port, he could almost sight an army of oil rigs digging deep into the Pacific sea.

Felix arrived at Port Verne in a shimmering Volkswagen driven by his friend, the hotel owner. The man came out and exclaimed, "Good evening folks! My name is Jerry. I am so terribly sorry for all that has happened to you, it's really a shame, truly. I should let you know that you all are very lucky, though; today, many of my guests left the Pioneer Inn. I would be so glad to host the survivors of hurricane Ten, the storm of the century. By golly, I might even get myself in the local newspaper! Hehehe."

Jerry had already appointed eight or so carriages to drive to and from the hotel to transport all of the people.

The Pioneer Inn, as the Wesleys learned, was established in the late nineteenth century as a safe haven for immigrants and sailors in search of a new home; this story was ironic in the boys' opinion, considering their situation and all. The hotel interior showcased a marvelous brick wall. Fluffy, navy-blue rugs covered the floor's various scratches and dents. The place was spacious, and the refugees were so very grateful to be hosted free of charge. All Jerry asked is that the guests would maintain clean shoes as they walked about the inn.

Most of the Sub Port residents had family or friends in the West Coast area, so these left on taxis and buses to get home before Christmas Eve. Others wished to stay; the place was so inviting and the company, friendly, that leaving without another place to stay seemed ridiculous.

Jack came into his room with his brother and his father. A weathered painting of a sailboat hung above a cot. Although the curtains were somewhat moldy, they could open to a magnificent view of the California ocean.

John left to speak to Jerry. Jack was tired, not because of a lack of sleep, but a need for a bed which would not rock and sway with the haphazard motion of the ocean. In a desk drawer, Sam found a Bible and a nursery rhyme book. He read, "Wynken, Blynken, and Nod one night sailed off in a wooden shoe—sailed on a river of crystal light into a sea of dew."

~

Five days later, on Christmas morning, Jerry invited the immigrants and retired workers to a wonderful breakfast. A dense, green Christmas tree decorated with all sorts of blue ornaments sparkled in the living quarters as *Emanuel* played on vinyl in the kitchen.

"My wife," said Jerry, "made the recipe for this main dish. I certainly hope that you enjoy it as much as I do. Hehe!"

Before eating, Pete the grocer asked to pray. He then thanked God for His grace and His love and asked for the food to nourish the guests. The people ate with grateful heart and cheerful spirits. Even Incandium's employees cracked smiles and enjoyed each other's company.

Without a Christmas stocking or present, each child found himself perfectly satisfied at the inn that day; the gift of survival and a safe place to stay was plenty.

Chad, Jack, and Lucy spent the day playing with the hotel radio system.

"This is Thrush, I am calling to alert you that a storm is headed your way," Lucy declared "prepare your hotel for evacuation, over!"

Chad responded, "This is Puffin. Mind me, this is the worst storm I have ever seen. How will we ever come out alive? Over!"

"This is Jay. We can escape," Jack said, giggling, "if we hurry to Port Verne fast enough, we could get away. You know, the bottom of the ocean is a safe place to stay during such a storm. Over and out!"

Then, the three burst out in laughter.

Later, Lucy asked Jack about how he was dealing with all that had happened. "It's sure a shame," Jack said thoughtfully, "but, I'm not as grieved as I had imagined I would be. Mr Berkley was a hero, and he seemed at peace with his choice. And now, my father is back, and that's what he had wanted all along."

It was on the twenty-sixth of December that a memorial for Mr Berkley was held. The large crowd came out from the Pioneer Inn on that rainy morning. In a grassy park beside the inn, the men, women, and children gathered to place lily flowers on the grass. The flowers rested beside a small plaque that read, "We will forever remember the life of a lighthouse operator who helped save the people of Genoa island when they needed him most."

John spoke of his friend: "David the King once wrote, 'If I take the wings of the morning, and dwell in the uttermost parts of the sea; even there shall thy hand lead me, and thy right hand shall hold me.' I cannot even begin to imagine–" the grey-haired man stopped for he could no longer find the words to say.

Jack stepped up from behind his father. With

fervor, he said to the crowd, "Mr Berkley was my friend and he is my inspiration. I remember this particular morning when he told me that he found rest in knowing that he had a purpose. Mr Berkley showed me what it looked like to have such a purpose. When I was afraid to go into a scary and unknown place, he would come along and make it pleasant. And he faced his fears for the sake of others."

John was trying to hide his tears by making good use of his handkerchief. He refused to speak anymore, and signaled for Jerry.

The hotel owner, who was an elder at the local church and hosting the memorial, said softly, "May God cherish this sea-fearing hero that He has blessed us with for many years."

The rain suddenly stopped and John stopped his crying. Sam appeared saddened, yet he kept his composure. Little rays of sunlight fell upon all who stood in the field. It was a special moment.

After placing a string of lilies beside the plaque, Mr Thompson said to John, "I will never forget the friend I had. Neither will I forget the adventure he brought us on. I assure you that there could have been no better man to watch over your two sons than David."

"Thank you, Clive." John said, as the man proceeded towards the ocean.

Lucy left later in the day to find a new Southern home. Jack was saddened to hear that she would no longer live in Oregon.

"It's a shame, I really liked her," Jack told Chad as they walked along a shell-coated beach, "I suppose your parents still want to live near Lyn Field?"

"I believe so," Chad said, putting his hood on, "my mother says there's a lot of land for sale out there."

~

After selling some stocks and making a down payment, John moved his sons into a new home. It was not a home on the shoreline, nor was it a home beneath the waves, but a cozy, wooden place found between a mountain and grassy field.

While living at his new home, Jack would spend his early mornings at the nearby ranch, sometimes with his father, sometimes with his brother. He would watch the strong horses eating and wandering on the rolling hills.

He would also look at the rough ocean from a distance. Genoa was a small dot on a clear day. The whispers in the wind and the murmurs from the cold river brought him peace. These things reminded him of sea-side tree-forts and games on a different western shore.

"I miss Genoa." stated Chad while visiting the Wesley residence one evening. The boy's parents had bought a property nearby, allowing he and Jack to spend time together on most days.

"So do I," Jack replied, "but I don't mind this life either."

"Ever think you'll go back?"

The fireplace roared and Sam's stew smelled wonderful.

"I know I will."

Chapter Twelve
1952

Jack and Sam were soon going to the public school near Lyn Field Bay. They made new friends and went on new adventures. The coastline near their home was much more industrialized than Genoa's, but it was alluring nonetheless. Jack's new friends invited him to volleyball games on the beach, and Sam was toured through different seaside caves by his classmates.

The dark-haired Wesley brother, now sixteen years old, enjoyed camping with his father on the weekends. Sitting beside a little fire, they would stay awake for hours. Jack loved to tell his father about the past winter's events. And John loved to listen, although he occasionally fell asleep during his son's recounting.

It was not long before Jack had written a story in his late-mother's hard-cover journal. He made sure to describe, in great detail, the events that took place at the Sub Port. He made Mr Berkley the hero of the story, as he ought to have been.

Sam was accepted into a university in Colorado, and, although Jack was terrified of a life without his best friend, he accepted new challenges, the good and the bad.

~

John's coat fluttered in a salty breeze as he stood on the polished wood platform. The new boat exceeded their expectations. The Wesleys were joined by Captain Wheaton Edwards as they jetted across Pacific waters.

John was overjoyed to feel the warm summer sun today—a day he had missed so wholly while he had been at the Sub Port. A school of flying fish skipped across the water nearby and Sam remarked that a cloud in the sky looked like an S.A.P.

"What on earth is an S.A.P.?" Captain Edwards inquired, squinting at the pointy cloud.

"Nothing good," John answered, "just a strange machine that could make you eggs or shoot you dead." He laughed heartily.

The tiny dot on the horizon soon became a green and grey protrusion—an island. Sam brought binoculars to his eyes and looked towards the dark-blue and yellow sails that darted across glimmering water. The air smelled of seaweed.

Coming to the port, the four viewed mounds of wood and other debris coating overturned docks. A few men were squatting in the area, digging through things, salvaging framed photographs and expensive instruments. "Genoa was a beautiful island," stated John, "if we had never come, it wouldn't look so bad now."

The strip of homes by the bay was utterly demolished. Wooden posts were ripped to bits, furniture was found in strange places.

Jack placed a cracked clock in a basket–a basket soon filled with old things of sentimental value: a vase, some jewelry having belonged to Marie, some unbroken china, and some colorful coats that stayed intact inside of a metal cabinet.

Jack thought once more of his life on Genoa; despite the dreary weather, he had always had much to do. He looked down at an old banner that read "THE WESLEY LIBRARY."

"I want to see the lighthouse." Sam said.

"I'll come with you." Jack replied.

The two dropped their findings at the collective heap and started eastward.

Hurricane Ten had struck Genoa Island with immeasurable power. But, a greater power had held together the fragile bond of family.

Jack walked by the hill he and his brother had camped on the day the telegram arrived. He was nervous, yet excited. He began to run. Sam ran as well.

Birds whistled a mysterious melody as the Wesley brothers beheld an amazing sight. Protruding from sun-bleached rocks stood the red and white lighthouse. It had stayed where it was on the white rock. It was still gleaming, and in quite perfect shape.

Josiah Swanson
On Sub-Marine

I spent much of my childhood in my imagination. Having grown fond of architecture, I dreamt of one day building an underwater hotel. Due to lack of patience and construction equipment, I began building the hotel with my brothers–in our minds. After completing the hotel's construction, we stayed there for months at a time, studying sea creatures and building robots. Somewhere along the way, I came up with the idea of writing a story about two brothers who came to stay at a similar hotel when a terrible storm struck the coast on which they lived. For several years I worked on the story until finally I decided I would make it a book. With help from my mom and some friends, I crafted the finished novella, Sub-Marine.

44714520R00086

Made in the USA
San Bernardino, CA
21 July 2019